"Clarke's Arrogance"

Manuel A. Ruiz Sosa

Translated by: Michelle Moore

1

About the Author: Manuel A. Ruiz Sosa

The author of the epic fantasy children's story "The Children and the Green Dragon," aimed at all ages, now brings us this new tale focused on a more mature audience. It is a blend of the author's love for fantastical stories and magical worlds, intertwined with his real-life experiences as a psychologist and an immigrant who became an air conditioning technician.

Born from the author's experiences in the world of air conditioning, this book is inspired by the incredible invention that has revolutionized human comfort. From the chilled bliss of a home conditioned to our desires to the simple pleasure of a cold drink on a hot day.

Grounded in the author's academic background in psychology and a deep love of literature, this narrative aims to not only entertain but also to educate. It invites readers to contemplate the complex interplay between personal, professional, and familial commitments.

Manuel A. Ruiz Sosa presents this tale as his second literary work, this time focused on an adult audience.

Dedication:

First that all, this English edition of this story is dedicated to the person that make it possible and put her translation skills to make it happen. Thank you, Michelle Moore, for helping this story to reach other horizons and to be known by more people.

I dedicate this book and story to my father, Carlos Ruiz. His insistence in my teenage years to read books that left a positive message and a lasting teaching, pushed me to create one for myself, based on my experience as a reader, psychologist and his great support as editor of this work.

I also dedicate it to my mother, Monica Sosa, her great support since my first stories written when I was a child have allowed me to continue believing in myself and polishing this skill that I use in my passion for writing.

To my wife, Catherine Flautero, for her support in all aspects of life, including those days when, due to long work hours as an air conditioning technician, she took care of keeping our home running smoothly and made time for my writing.

To my sons, Gabriel and Ethan Ruiz, so that they may always remain humble and be willing to work as a team and support each other in achieving their goals.

To my sister, Monica Ruiz, who has always been by my side on my adventures and provided me with different perspectives on life.

To my aunt Luisa, my second mother, who has always supported me in all my endeavors and was also one of my first readers, offering recommendations to enrich my stories.

To Gustavo Terrero, your advice over the years has allowed me to see things with a wider threshold and to make many good decisions. I hope this book inspires you to make the literary project you want to write.

To my uncle Chicho, better known as Dr. Francisco Sosa Cabeza, an inspiration to me both as a medical professional and as a writer. I still enjoy and share the excitement of bringing this collection of ideas and words to life in a book, just as he has done with his 12 years of experience and four published volumes.

To my father-in-law, Ignacio Flautero, who during my years as a psychology student always recommended me to learn and study technical trade and invest in tools. Today I can see the value of his advice in having two totally different professions that have opened horizons of understanding for me and have allowed me to bring them together to not only live from them; but to create this fantastic experience.

To my brother-in-law, Carlos Flautero, as a professional on the air conditioning, he was the reason why I got in volve in that trade and it world.

I also dedicate this story to my colleagues and mentors in the air conditioning and refrigeration industry. While it was never a career, I imagined myself in, I've discovered it to be a unique calling and service. It has broadened my horizons, teaching me to appreciate the everyday miracles, like the comfort of air conditioning in a Florida summer. I admire those who work tirelessly to provide this essential service.

Index:

1. An Exceptional Worker   7

2. Reaching the Limit   18

3. The Weight of Decisions   27

4. Welcome to Zal   37

5. The Village of Zira   49

6. The Mine of Magic Crystals   61

7. Do Something Useful   73

8. The Risky Quest   87

9. A Miraculous Idea   99

10. Let's Get to Work   115

11. It's a Team Effort   134

12. Each to their own Trade   149

13. Threads in the Shadows   162

14. Unexpected Allies   176

15. Bad Intentions   197

16. Guardian Angel   223

17. The Final Stretch   239

18. A New Man   254

Chapter 1: An Exceptional Worker

Clarke woke up to the sound of his alarm clock. It was six in the morning, and the sun was already starting to warm the sky. He got out of bed and went to the bathroom. He showered, shaved, and got dressed in his blue CoolForever uniform, the largest and most prestigious air conditioning company in Florida.

He was CoolForever's "Master Tech," the most experienced and respected technician in the company. With over thirty years in the industry, there wasn't an air conditioning problem he couldn't solve. He took great pride in his work and always believed in doing things himself. He didn't trust the new, inexperienced technicians who had recently joined the company. He considered them incompetent and lazy. He personally handled the most difficult and demanding cases and wouldn't let anyone help him or tell him how to do his job.

Clarke left his house and got into his white pickup truck, which was full of tools and spare parts. He started the engine and headed to the CoolForever headquarters, where his boss, Mr. Jones, was waiting for him. Mr. Jones was the owner and founder of CoolForever, and he had hired Clarke when he was just a young apprentice. Clarke respected and was loyal to him, but he was also irritated by his way of running the company. Mr. Jones was an older man who had fallen behind in technological advances and still did things the old-fashioned way. Clarke thought the company needed to modernize and adapt to the new times, but Mr. Jones refused to listen to his suggestions.

Clarke arrived at the office and greeted Mr. Jones, who was sitting behind his desk. Mr. Jones returned the greeting and handed him a folder with the day's service orders.

—Good morning, Clarke. The team has a very busy schedule today. There are many customers who need their air conditioning fixed. The summer is very hot, and people can't stand the heat. You must be quick and do a good job as always. Remember, customer satisfaction is the most important thing.
—Don't worry, Mr. Jones. I'll take care of everything. I'm the best technician this company has, and there's nothing I can't handle. I don't need anyone to help me or supervise me. I know what I'm doing.

—That's great, Clarke. I appreciate your confidence and professionalism. But don't forget that you're not alone. You have a team of technicians who work with you and who can lend a hand if you need it. Don't be so proud and accept help from others. That way you can get more work done and faster.

—Thanks for the advice, Mr. Jones. But I prefer to work alone. The other technicians just get in my way and waste my time. They don't know what they're doing, and they just create more problems for me. I'm the Master Tech and nobody can teach me anything.

Clarke grabbed the folder and headed to his truck. Mr. Jones watched him go, a mix of admiration and concern in his eyes. He knew Clarke was a great technician, but he also knew his attitude was a problem. Mr. Jones planned to retire soon and make Clarke the manager, but he feared that Clarke, in that position, would have many jobs and problems that he wouldn't know how to solve and that his pride would prevent him from asking for help. Mr. Jones hoped that when that day came, Clarke would be ready, as he was very intelligent.

Clarke left the office and got started. He had several clients to visit who had called CoolForever for air conditioning repairs. Clarke looked at the folder and saw that he had to go to a house, a restaurant, an office, and a hotel. The jobs were of varying complexity and duration, but Clarke was not afraid of any of them. He could fix any type of air conditioning, from the oldest to the most modern.

He arrived at the first address, which was a house in a residential neighborhood. He rang the doorbell, and an elderly lady opened the door, greeting him with a smile.

—Good morning, sir. You must be the technician from CoolForever. Thank you for coming so quickly. My air conditioning isn't working and I'm very hot.

—Good morning, Ma'am. I'm Clarke, the Master Tech from CoolForever. Don't worry, I'll fix the problem in a moment. Where is the unit?

—It's in the living room, next to the sofa. Please come in.

Clarke entered the house and went to the living room. He saw the air conditioner, which was an old and noisy model. He examined it and saw that the filter was dirty and the unit was frozen over. Clarke took out his tools and got to work. He changed the filter, defrosted the unit, and cleaned it. In less than two hours, the air conditioner was working again and began to cool the room

—There you go, ma'am. Your air conditioner is as good as new. Now you can enjoy a cool and comfortable climate.

—Oh, thank you so much, Mr. Clarke! You're an angel. How much do I owe you?

—Nothing, ma'am. The service is included as part of your CoolForever membership. You just need to sign here.

— Of course, Mr. Clarke. Here you go. And here, this is for you, some water and a snack. You must be hungry after working so hard.

—No, thank you, ma'am. I don't have time to eat. I must go to other places. I appreciate the gesture, but I can't accept it.

—Come on, Mr. Clarke. Don't be so hard on yourself. You must take care of yourself and eat well. Work is important, but your health is more important.

—Don't worry about me, ma'am. I'm fine. I'm tough and resilient. Work is my life and I never get tired of it. Goodbye, ma'am. Have a nice day.

Clarke left the house and climbed into his truck. Ignoring the woman's offer, he drove off. Clarke never ate or drank on the job. He thought it was a waste of time and that it made him less efficient. He preferred to work nonstop, giving his all and doing more detailed work than most.

As usual, Clarke set his GPS and headed to his next call. He drove to the next destination, a restaurant. He parked his truck and went inside. He approached the counter and asked for the owner.

—Good morning, sir. I'm Clarke, the Master Tech from CoolForever. I'm here to repair your air conditioning.

—Good morning, Mr. Clarke. I'm the owner of the restaurant. Thank you for coming so quickly. The air conditioning unit is in the kitchen and it's not cooling at all. The cooks are sweating like crazy and the customers are complaining about the heat.

—Don't worry, sir. I'll have it fixed in no time. Where is the kitchen?

—It's at the back, to the right. Just follow the arrows.

Clarke followed the directions and arrived in the kitchen. He saw the air conditioner, a large and powerful model. He examined it and saw that the thermostat was broken, the fan was jammed, and the electrical circuit was damaged. Clarke took out his tools and got to work. In the middle of all this, his son called:

—Hi Dad, how are you? — his son said in a cheerful voice.

—Busy, Alejandro, what's up?' Clarke replied, focused on the machine he was working on

—No, nothing happened, Dad. I just wanted to know if you were getting off early today so you could come watch the football game with me this afternoon— Alejandro said excitedly.

—Alejandro, you know I can't. Work never stops in the summer and the customers are waiting. We can watch it recorded another time, son — Clarke replied, eager to cut the conversation short and get back to work.

—Okay, Dad. I'll record it and we'll watch it later - Alejandro said, his voice filled with disappointment. He knew this was the usual response, and he doubted they'd ever get around to watching the game together.

—Alright, son. Good to hear from you. Talk to you later — Clarke replied before hanging up. He returned his focus to the task at hand.

Clarke didn't like being called on the phone in the middle of his work, just like this call. He constantly interrupted conversations to focus on what he was doing. His job was dangerous and he had to be attentive to avoid accidents. But even outside of work, at night, he didn't call back because he arrived home tired from his long workday and left his personal phone with accumulated unread messages, emails, and voice notes.

Continuing with his work in the restaurant, Clarke replaced the thermostat, unclogged the fan, and repaired the circuit. In less than an hour, the air conditioner was working again and began to cool the room.

—There you go, sir. Your air conditioner is good as new. Now you can enjoy a cool and pleasant climate.

—Oh, thank you so much, Mr. Clarke! You're a genius. How much do I owe you?

—Nothing, sir. The service is included in the CoolForever warranty. You just must sign here.

— Of course, Mr. Clarke. Excellent service.

Clarke left the restaurant, pleased with another satisfied customer, and climbed into his truck.

He continued his workday, which had started early in the morning and continued customer after customer until nightfall.

For his last jobs, Clarke pushed himself to maintain the same level of quality and continue to provide excellent service, but without taking any breaks in between and sometimes even holding in the urge to go to the bathroom so as not to deviate from his work routes. Clarke knew he was an exceptional worker who worked longer hours than average, and his pride made him feel good to know that at the end of the day. But everything has a price, and so much demand without care was taking its toll on his body, his mental health, and his social life.

He didn't realize it, but his workload was unsustainable and was causing him stress, fatigue, and isolation. At almost 50, he felt like he was 70. His hair was gray, his skin wrinkled, and his eyes were bloodshot. His back and knees ached, his stomach burned, and his head pounded.

Clarke had no friends, was divorced, and saw his son less and less. His job was all he had. He denied being unwell, but after cold showers at night, lying in bed staring at the ceiling, the deafening silence of loneliness would overwhelm him. He'd drown it out with sleeping pills, a good pillow, and dreams of becoming the company's new manager. He imagined everything would be much easier once he was in the office and could finally make time for exercise, spending time with his son, and training other technicians.

Chapter 2: Reaching the Limit

Several months passed with Clarke's life going on as usual, until the day he had been eagerly anticipating finally arrived. Mr. Jones, ready to retire after a long career at the company, decided to pass the managerial role on to Clarke, who had always strived to reach this position. As the days went by after taking over, Clarke started to realize that the transition from being a field technician interacting with clients to sitting in an office managing a team was more challenging than he had expected.

Clarke was sitting in his new office, which had previously belonged to Mr. Jones. He felt proud and honored by the trust that Mr. Jones had placed in him, but he also felt overwhelmed and stressed by the responsibility that came with the position.

He was no longer just a technician, but also a leader. He had to manage a team of over twenty technicians, who depended on him for service orders, spare parts, tools, instructions, advice, and support. Clarke had to organize the work, assign tasks, supervise results, solve problems, address complaints, negotiate with suppliers, report to the director, and satisfy customers. Clarke had to do all of that and more. Sometimes he even wanted to jump into a service van and go to customers' homes to repair the air conditioning machines that some of his technicians found difficult, and that he wanted to fix better than anyone else.

Clarke wanted to be a good boss, but he didn't know how. His pride got in the way of delegating tasks and trusting his team. Clarke still thought he was the best technician and that others were not capable of doing things as well as he did. He still wanted to do things himself and would not accept help or the opinion of anyone. Despite his tireless efforts and attention to detail, his approach was causing significant problems.

Clarke had earned the dislike and resentment of his subordinates, who saw him as an authoritarian, demanding, and arrogant boss. He didn't listen to them, he didn't value them, he didn't motivate them, or recognize them, he didn't train them and didn't support them. Instead, he only criticized them, pressured them, punished them, humiliated, ignored, exploited and despised his team. Clarke was not a leader, but a tyrant.

He had also earned the distrust and concern of his superiors, who saw him as an inefficient, inflexible, and isolated boss. For them, he was not a good employee for that role but was beginning to be a problem.

Meanwhile, Clarke's clients were becoming increasingly dissatisfied. They saw him as an irresponsible, indifferent, and very difficult manager to contact. If he didn't have another technician on the phone to supervise what they were doing, you could find him with his hands busy repairing a machine, intervening in the work of another technician because he felt he could do it better.

Clarke was so busy that he didn't realize everything he was doing wrong. He was demanding even more of himself than in previous years of his career, but he wasn't getting the results he expected. Clarke was losing control, quality, reputation, respect, trust, credibility, and profitability.

It didn't take long for the company to land a big commercial contract with one of the city's buildings. As manager of the CoolForever air department, Clarke had a duty to ensure that the installation of an air conditioning system that would supply conditioned spaces to the entire building was carried out in the best possible way, with an efficient team that would perform the installation in a professional and safe manner.

That day, Clarke had arrived early with his truck, tools, and materials. He started work half an hour early, and as the normal working hours approached, his technicians began to arrive. None of them had a good face; they knew it would be one of those long days where Clarke wouldn't let the other technicians work unless it was his way and at his pace.

Thus, the installation proceeded, with a large team of workers and heavy machinery on several floors of the building. Clarke was constantly moving between teams and areas to supervise the work and almost always intervened. He criticized, humiliated, and contradicted the technicians when they deviated from the original plan and contributed new ideas.

As the week progressed, Clarke's team had made significant headway on the large installation project. With only Friday left to complete the electrical connections, they were almost finished.

That Friday, Clarke arrived early as usual, eager to get started. However, as the clock ticked by, he realized that none of his team had shown up. Growing impatient, he decided to call one of them.

—Where are you? I'm waiting. We need to finish the machine today. It's urgent.

—Sorry, boss. I'm not coming in.

—What do you mean you're not coming? What's wrong with you?

—Nothing, boss. I've had enough.

—Enough of what? What are you talking about?

—I'm saying that I can no longer tolerate your management style. Your behavior towards us is unacceptable. You constantly demand more of us than is reasonable, criticize our work unfairly, and humiliate us in front of clients. You disregard our requests for time off and frequently threaten termination. You show us no respect or appreciation. You're a tyrant.

—That's not true. I'm a good boss. I just want you to do your job well. I just want you to be professional. I just want you to be like me.

—Well, we don't want to be like you, boss. You're obsessive, a loner, and bitter. You have no life, no friends, no family. You only have your job. And your job is killing you. You're sick, boss. And you're making us sick.

—Don't talk nonsense. I'm fine. I'm strong and resilient. I'm the best technician there is. I can do any job. I don't need anyone.

— Then do it yourself, boss, because I'm not going to work with you anymore. Neither am I, nor any of the others. We've decided to quit. We've found another job. In a company that treats us better. That respects us, values us, helps us. That makes us feel part of a team.

— Are you serious? How could you all quit? What am I supposed to do now? Who will finish the installation?

—I don't know, Clarke. I don't care. It's not my problem. Goodbye.

The technician hung up the phone. Clarke held the phone in his hand, unable to believe what he had just heard. His technicians had abandoned him. They had left him alone. They had betrayed him.

He felt a mix of anger, sadness, and fear. Anger at the disloyalty of his technicians, sadness at the loss of his coworkers, and fear for his uncertain future. But Clarke didn't let those emotions defeat him. He suppressed them and replaced them with another: pride.

He told himself he didn't need anyone. As the Master Tech, he was more than capable of finishing the job alone. With newfound determination, he prepared to face the challenge, no matter how daunting.

Clarke stepped into the elevator and made his way to the cramped machine room, whit his heavy tool bag on his hand. It was a small space full of cables. He had to juggle to get through with all the materials. Then, he went down to the basement, where the electrical breakers were. He had to turn them off to be able to connect the machine without the risk of electrocution. Clarke turned off the breakers and went back up to the roof. He connected the machine and turned it on. Everything seemed to be working fine. Clarke smiled and congratulated himself. He had done it. Even if it took him up to 3 times as long as it would have taken him with the help of his technicians.

However, Clarke had made a fatal mistake. He had forgotten to turn the breakers back off and he didn't have anyone to check on him or warn him. When he was adjusting the final part of the air, he didn't realize that the cables were alive and it caused a terrible explosion.

The explosion was so loud it echoed throughout the building. Clarke screamed in pain and terror at the unexpected shock. As sparks flew from the short circuit, a blazing fire ignited and rapidly spread through the cramped machine room.

Injured by the fire and coughing from the smoke that filled the room, Clarke crawled and stumbled as best he could out of that infernal scene while suffering the intense pain of burns. He managed to reach another part of the roof where, covered in burn wounds, he watched as the machine room at the other end was consumed by flames. Clarke had never had such a dangerous or near-fatal accident. He was shocked by his carelessness and disappointed. This was probably the end of his life, if not his career.

The pain coursing through his body was unbearable; even breathing was an agony. He was uncertain of the severity of his injuries and worried about his future. The smoke he'd inhaled left him gasping for air. Within minutes, lying on the floor, Clarke lost consciousness. As his vision faded, he heard the distant wail of sirens as ambulances and firefighters arrived.

Chapter 3: The Weight of Decisions

Clarke opened his eyes and found himself in a hospital room. He was surrounded by tubes, wires, and machines that kept him alive. He couldn't move. And slowly he started to be available to see, hear, speak with difficulty, and think.

He saw a doctor who approached his bed. The doctor looked at him with a compassionate expression and spoke to him in a soft voice.

— Good morning, Mr. Clarke. I'm glad you're awake. You've been in a coma for two weeks. You've been in a serious accident. There was an explosion in the building where you were working. You were installing an air conditioning unit. Do you remember?

Clarke remembered. He remembered the job, the machine, the wires, the mistake, the explosion. He remembered the pain, the fear, the loneliness, the danger of death. He remembered everything.

— I know this is difficult to accept, Mr. Clarke. But I must tell you the truth. You've lost both of your hands and legs. You also have severe burns over much of your body, and other internal injuries. You've survived by a miracle. Thanks to the firefighters and paramedics who rescued you, you're still with us.

Clarke felt a mix of relief, sadness, and anger. Relief for having survived. Sadness for having lost his limbs. Anger for having caused the accident. It couldn't be that he hardly ever made a mistake, and now he was facing the consequences of one that had nearly taken his life. He couldn't believe it.

— Don't worry, Mr. Clarke— the doctor reassured him. —You're not alone. We're here to help you. You're going to receive the best possible treatment. You're going to have prosthetics, physical therapy, and psychological support. You're going to recover. You're going to live again.

Clarke didn't believe the doctor. He thought his life was over and that there was nothing left to live for. He could no longer work, and without his full independence at nearly 50 years old, he felt like he could do very little.

The doctor stood near the door and said to Clarke — I understand that this is a lot to take in at once. I'm going to leave you alone, and a group of nurses will be monitoring your recovery. Don't worry, we've contacted your family and they're aware of what's happened— The doctor then left and closed the door.

In the deep silence and solitude of the room, Clarke thought back on all the decisions he had made in his life. He realized how prioritizing work above everything else had led him to this point. How his pride and refusal to accept help or delegate had affected him. How he had lost everything that mattered to him.

Clarke thought of his ex-wife, who had left him because he worked too much and didn't pay attention to her. He remembered his son, who had resented him for not being there and not supporting him. He thought of his parents, who had died without him visiting or calling them. He remembered his friends, who had abandoned him for not wanting to socialize or have fun. He thought of his technicians, who had betrayed him for not respecting or valuing them. He remembered his clients, who had sued him for not attending to their needs as manager. He thought of his job, which had consumed and destroyed him because he didn't make the balance even when the company offered the support.

Clarke regretted everything he had done wrong. He lamented everything he had lost. He hated himself. Clarke cried. He cried like he had never cried before. He cried like a child. He cried until he fell asleep. Then he dreamed. He dreamed of a different life. A life where he would have been more humble, more generous, happier. A life where he would have had love, friendship, family. A life that would have made sense.

Clarke fell into a deep sleep, his tears a testament to the profound reflection on his life. He slept through the night and into the morning. In that deep sleep, there were no dreams, only a dark, silent void.

He woke up early the following morning. He opened his eyes and was met with surprise. In the chair near his bed, a person was taking sit, not his son as he had hoped to see, but an unknown man. He was an older gentleman, with white hair and a long white beard. He looked like a wise Chinese sage. He was wearing a gray suit, a white shirt, and a red tie. He had a kind smile and a deep gaze.

—Good morning, Mr. Clarke. I'm glad to see you're awake. I'm Doctor Lee. I'm the hospital psychiatrist. I'm here to help you.

—Good morning, Doctor Lee. Psychiatrist? What are you doing here? Who called you?

—No one called me. I came on my own initiative. I've read your file and it seemed to me that you needed to talk to someone. Someone who understands you and can offer advice.

—I don't need to talk to anyone, Doctor Lee. I don't need anyone to understand me or give me advice. I don't need your help.

—Don't be so proud, Mr. Clarke. Pride is a virtue, but it's also a flaw. Pride that became in arrogance has brought you here, but it can also take you out of here. It depends on how you use it.

—I don't know what you're talking about. I don't know what you want from me.

—I want to help you; I want you to recover. I want you to start living again.

—Start living again? For what? What's the point of my life?

—Your life has the meaning that you want to give it, Mr. Clarke. You can choose between continuing to suffer or starting to enjoy. You can choose between isolating yourself or connecting with others. You can choose between hating yourself or loving yourself.

—I have no choice. I have nothing. I have no hands, no legs, no job, no family, no friends. I have nothing.

—Yes, you do, Mr. Clarke. You have many things. You have your mind, your heart, your soul. You have your past, your present, your future. You have your opportunity, your challenge, your destiny.

—I don't understand what you're saying.

—I'll explain it to you. You have a privileged mind. You are intelligent, creative, ingenious. You can learn, invent, solve. You can use your mind to do wonderful things. Things that will make you and others happy.

—How can I use my mind, Doctor Lee? How can I do those wonderful things you're talking about?

—You can use your mind to read, to write, to draw, to compose, to teach, to inspire, to dream. You can do wonderful things with your mind, Mr. Clarke. You just have to start.

—I don't know, Doctor, I might enjoy those things, but I don't think they'll make me happy. I don't know if I can be happy again. I don't even know where to start or how to do it.

—You can do it with the help of your heart, Mr. Clarke. Your heart is a force that allows you to feel, to get excited, to connect. You can use your heart to forgive, to ask for forgiveness, to give thanks, to apologize, to compliment, to recognize, to respect, to help, to accept help, to give, to receive, to share, to trust, to delegate, to lead, to follow, to listen, to speak, to understand, to empathize, to love, to be loved. You can use your heart for whatever you want, you just have to open it.

— And how can I open it?

—You can open it with the desire to do so, but that alone won't be enough. You'll need to keep it open, and for that, I've brought you this incense. This incense is magical. It has the power to transport you to another place. A place full of challenges, but where anything is possible. A world where you can be whoever you want to be. A world where you can do whatever you want to do and where you can live however you want to live. A world where you can try to learn what you haven't learned here if you truly want to open your heart.

—What are you saying, Doctor Lee? What is that incense? What is that world?

—It's a secret, Mr. Clarke. A secret that life will reveal to you. A secret that you will reveal to yourself. It's an opportunity to start over and to redeem yourself. An opportunity to live.

—I don't understand.

—You don't have to understand it, Mr. Clarke. You just have to accept it. You just have to try it. What I'm bringing you is an opportunity to recover from lost time and make different decisions that will lead you to a better life. But I must warn you, you can only return to this world after one year and when it ends, you must have given to others what you didn't give in this world. If you don't succeed, all this will pass like a dream and you will be back here whit nothing.

Clarke didn't quite understand everything Doctor Lee had explained to him. There was a lot of mysticism involved, and Clarke had never had time to believe in anything other than his own abilities, science, and his work. However, his situation had him desperate and in a state of grief where reality and fiction made little sense to him.

— What do you say, Clarke, do you accept the challenge?

—I've never said no to a challenge, Mr. Lee, but I don't quite understand what you expect of me in this state. I don't fully understand your challenge or how I can recover from this. I don't know if I want to continue. But go ahead, do what you must do. Maybe that incense of yours has some psychotropic properties that will help me forget all this, that would be helpful for a fresh start.

Doctor Lee was silent. He lit the incense and placed it on a small table next to Clarke's bed. The incense smoke spread through the room, filling the air with a sweet and intoxicating aroma.

Clarke breathed in the smoke and felt a sense of peace and joy. He closed his eyes and let himself be carried away by the scent. He felt as if he were floating and as if his soul was detaching from his body. He felt as if time had stopped and suddenly, he was just floating in a great void. Clarke stopped feeling any noise or presence, he only heard the sound of his own heart getting louder and louder. He calmed down and after a while fell asleep.

Chapter 4: Welcome to Zal

Clarke woke up to find himself sprawled on the sands of a desert. He was lying beneath a dead tree that shielded him from the intense heat of the sun. He got up and looked around. There was nothing but sand, rocks, and cacti. He rubbed his eyes and looked up at the sky. There were two suns. One was red, and the other was yellow. Clarke gaped in astonishment. He couldn't believe what he was seeing.

He touched his face and body. He realized that his hands and legs were unharmed. There was no trace of the injuries from the explosion he suffered before been at the hospital. Clarke felt more vigorous and his skin, although covered in sand, seemed less wrinkled and smoother. He realized he was several years younger. He had more hair, felt better, and all his old weaknesses had vanished. Clarke was amazed. He couldn't believe what he was feeling.

He remembered what had happened to him before. He remembered the accident, the hospital, Dr. Lee, the incense, the dream. He remembered everything. Clarke wondered where he was and what was happening. He felt confused and scared. He couldn't understand what was happening to him.

He decided to look for an explanation. He decided to wander through the desert, looking for any sign of life, a town, or a lake. He followed his instinct, hoping to find some answer. Could Dr. Lee have transported him to another place? Or was it a hallucination? Clarke had many doubts, but he wasn't going to sit around waiting with the scorching heat beating down on his body.

Clarke walked through the desert for a couple of hours. He found nothing and no one, just sand, rocks and the two suns, which burned his skin and blinded his sight. He became dehydrated and tired. He despaired and little by little his spirits were consumed until he felt exhausted on the hot sands. Trying to catch his breath and using the little energy he had left, he sat on the ground and resigned himself to dying. He wasn't sure if it was all a psychotropic effect of the incense or a bad dream, of those that seem too real until you wake up. This couldn't be real; he must be in a trance or something. Perhaps, if he let himself die, he would wake up again in the hospital. One way or another, Clarke felt really fucked up, listless and depressed.

But then, Clarke heard a bark. He lifted his head looking for the source of the noise and saw a dog. It was a desert dog. It looked like a mix between a dog and a hyena. It had short brown hair, long pointed ears, a short curly tail, and bright black eyes. Its size was much larger than an average dog. This dog/hyena approached Clarke and sniffed him. Then, it spoke to him.

— Hello, human. What are you doing here? Are you lost?

Clarke was stunned. The dog was talking to him. In words. With sense. Clarke didn't know what to say. He didn't know what to do. He thought he had already gone crazy and deranged.

—Don't be scared. I'm not going to hurt you. I'm just passing through the desert and couldn't avoid seeing you lying there all sad. My name is

Rex. And you? What are you doing here? Is everything alright?

Clarke gathered his courage and replied.

—My name is Clarke. I'm here because... the truth is I don't know what I'm doing here, or how I got here, or where I am. All I know is that this desert is nothing like anything I've seen in Florida. I don't know what's going on.

—I see, Clarke. You're confused. You're in the Zal desert. It's a bad place to wander around alone, without crystals and especially with those clothes— said Rex, looking at Clarke strangely and contemptuously.

Clarke hadn't realized he was still wearing his hospital gown, which, as usual, left his entire rear end exposed.

— Umm... let's not talk about my clothes, okay?— said Clarke, embarrassed and covering himself most as he can.— Then he continued — What do you say, Rex? What is the Zal desert? How is it that you can talk or how is it that I can understand you?

Rex looked at him strangely —The sun must have gotten to you, Clarke, you're a very strange human, although what human isn't? All Sharq can speak the common language in case you didn't know — said Rex ironically, referring to "Sharq" as the race of creature to which he belonged —Follow me, Clarke, I'm heading through the desert and I'm sure we can find some shade or a place to rest until we reach my village.

With few options left, confused and parched beyond belief, Clarke decided to follow this strange, talkative dog down the path.

They wandered for hours through the scorching desert dunes. Rex, who seemed like a city dog and walked with effort but was accustomed to it, never stopped talking, telling Clarke all about the desert and his adventures there.

Clarke wasn't much of a listener. He was used to doing all the talking in his professional circles, where he usually boasted about his expertise. Now he was lost, knew nothing about the place, and his only hope was to follow this talking dog who was spinning all sorts of tales, none of which Clarke cared about at the moment.

—Well, that's how I discovered as a pup that sand wasn't food and that it was hard to get off your tongue—Rex finished one of his tales.

—How much longer until we find water?—Clarke asked, parched and nearly melting from the heat.

—Just a little bit more, but don't despair, we're almost there.

Rex and Clarke kept walking until they reached a valley. It was a shady valley, and much cooler. There were trees, and in the center, you could see a pond of water. It was an oasis in the desert. It was paradise in the middle of hell.

Clarke's spirits lifted, his eyes widened like an owl's, and he began to imagine himself swimming and drinking from the lake, as well as cooling off in the shade provided by the trees and rocks.

— Clarke, we haven't reached it yet, don't even think about it— Rex said, warning him about that little valley.

— What do you mean, Rex? How can you say don't even think about it? If we've been walking for hours and haven't had a sip of water. This is perfect, this is amazing.

—No, Clarke, you're wrong. I have very good reasons to avoid that valley and keep going through the desert a little further to our destination.

—You're crazy, Rex, this is the perfect opportunity to get some water. You're just a dumb dog, so don't worry, if you don't want to come, I'll go and then catch up with you.

—Don't be reckless, Clarke. These valleys often seem too good to be true. Don't get distracted.

—I don't care, Rex. I don't care. I want to go into the valley. And I'm going to drink and cool off in that pond whether you like it or not.

Overwhelmed by thirst, pride, and curiosity, Clarke ignored Rex's warnings and headed towards the valley, eager to cool off in the lake. From a distance, Rex watched in disbelief at Clarke's recklessness and stubbornness.

Clarke reached the lake and without a second thought, he took a drink of its crystal-clear water. A wave of relief washed him over as the cool liquid slid down his throat. It was tasteless and felt quite clean. Desperate, Clarke drank deeply and even submerged himself in the water. He was overjoyed.

—That silly dog wanted me to miss out on this, on this wonder. I don't leave until I know exactly where we are going and how I carry water for the road. This lake is fantastic! — Clarke said to himself as he enjoyed the water and swam in it.

Clarke was so lost in thought about the valley lake, which had restored his energy and provided relief from the scorching heat of the Zal desert. He was so focused on drinking and refreshing his hair with the water that he didn't hear the very heavy footsteps in the sand that were slowly approaching him.

—Clarke! Get out of there, hurry! — Rex shouted from a distance.

Clarke laughed and submerged himself in the water, unable to hear Rex's warning shouts. On one of these submersions, when Clarke surfaced for air, he noticed some small creatures looking at him from the shore of the lake.

They were fire gnomes. These creatures are considered evil by most habitants of Zal. They were small and red, with horns, fangs, and claws. Their hair and eyes were fiery. They looked very angry and carried weapons like bows and short swords in their hands.

Clarke was startled to see these small, hostile creatures gathered on the shore, watching him, roaring, and brandishing their swords. In an instant, his heart raced because he knew he had been reckless and was now in danger.

In a flash, one of the fire gnomes prepared an arrow and fired at Clarke. The arrow grazed Clarke's left arm, leaving a small cut. Clarke grabbed the wound in pain and began to swim frantically away from the gnomes. They ran along the shore, following Clarke and continued to fire their arrows and spears.

When Clarke finally reached the shore at the other end, he began to run among the rocks of the valley, but the valley was bordered by stone corridors, some of which ended in dead ends. He was lost, with the only advantage being that the gnomes had very short legs and ran slowly with their heavy weapons.

Suddenly, Clarke heard a hopeful bark. It was Rex, calling him from a nearby area in the valley. Without hesitation, Clarke ran after him. Both companions moved swiftly through the labyrinth of rocks in the stone corridors, leaving behind the small fire gnomes who were burning hotter than usual due to Clarke and Rex's intrusion.

With skill and speed, both companions managed to escape the valley. Once they were safely away from it, back in the hot dunes of the desert, Clarke and Rex took a breath and looked back to see that the gnomes were no longer following them.

—Thanks, Rex, you saved me from whatever those creatures were. But this is crazy, why didn't you tell me there were monsters like that in the valley?

—I told you it was a bad idea to enter that valley, everyone knows there are fire gnomes in those places and they jealously guard those pools. It's like a sacred or cursed place for them.

—What? Are you telling me there are more like those creatures in other valleys?

—Of course, Clarke, hahaha you're really lost. Where are you from?

—I'm from the Earth, specifically the United States of America, Florida.

—Hmmm... that's strange, I don't know any place called like that, it must be very far away. Well, now that you're not going to run off to other valleys, you can follow me, we should be close to my village now.

Clarke and Rex continued their journey through the desert dunes. Now Clarke was clear that he was a stranger in a very distant land, like no one he had ever seen before, of which he knew nothing and was incredibly lucky to have encountered a talking dog, kind enough to guide him to a safe place. He understood that he would have to heed Rex's warnings if he wanted to stay alive and find a way to return to his world.

Perhaps he would have a mission to fulfill here, or something important to learn, he remembered Dr. Lee and his words, he only had one year to survive and give something to others that he never gave in his world of origin, he didn't know what exactly it was, but he had accepted the challenge and was trapped in it. Clarke decided to venture with Rex to see what the future held for him.

Chapter 5: The Village of Zira

Clarke and Rex wandered through the desert. Each step that sank into the hot sands made Clarke more and more desperate. He remembered how, back in Florida, during his job as a technician, he would endure the heat of summer while repairing air conditioning units or sweating profusely in attics. He knew he was used to the heat, but there was something about the Zal desert, with its two suns, that made the heat of his job feel milder than what he was experiencing now, especially with the scarcity of water and shade in the desert.

Rex, leading the way across the dunes, observed Clarke's lost expression and asked, — Hey Clarke, what are you thinking about?

Clarke didn't know how to respond. Explaining his job to a desert dog/hyena seemed too complicated, and his mouth was dry and full of sand, so he said the first thing that came to mind. — I'm thinking about how much longer do we need to walk until we reach your village.

—It won't be long now; I can already smell the Kuras from here.

—What are Kuras?

—My friend Clarke, the Kuras are the noblest animals in the desert, second only to the Sharq of course. Their meat is a bit tough but tasty, their milk is refreshing, they are strong and very useful to the villages, and when they die their shells make excellent homes for me and all the Sharq.

Clarke remembered that Sharq was what Rex called his race of "dogs/hyenas" and from the description, these Kura were some kind of very strange and large turtles.

The journey continued with Rex's tales about the time he got stuck in a Kura's shell and lived inside it for a month, surrounded by other Kuras, believing he had undergone some kind of metamorphosis until he managed to pry himself off the shell.

After several hours, Clarke began to see signs of civilization in the distance. Some stone walls with the color of sand, supported houses and huts. He could also see silhouettes of people in the distance and the giant, strange turtles that Rex called Kuras.

—Clarke, we're here. That over there is the Village of Zira. It's known for having people who work in the crystal mines and being a center of trade between the villages of Zal.

Clarke was amazed by what he was seeing and hearing about the village. As they got closer, Clarke noticed lights in lanterns connected to tubes of a strange metal, many human people in desert clothing, several burly dwarves, and other beings like humans but with long legs and pointed ears, very athletic. He also noticed a huge water fountain located at the entrance to the village, from which jets of water were gushing.

Clarke couldn't resist and ran ahead of Rex, quickly running to take water from that fountain. He submerged his head and took big gulps of water, rubbed it on his face and eyes. It was a great relief to be able to cool off after having been on the verge of despair during his journey through the scorching desert.

When Clarke lifted his head, his thirst quenched and everything covered in water from the tips of his hair to his feet, he noticed that Rex and the villagers nearby were looking at him with horror.

— What's wrong, Rex? Why is everyone looking at me like that?

— Uhh... Clarke, that's the Kura's water, and those animals drink the water and spit it out. Please don't do that or I'll have to say I don't know you and everyone will think you're crazy.

Clarke was surprised and realized he hadn't even noticed the grayish color of the water and the lumps floating in it. He felt a tremendous disgust and nausea. But he managed to hold it in for a moment.
— Come on, Clarke, you need a bath urgently, one for your body and another for your soul after this— Rex said with disgust.

They walked through the village, followed by the stares of the villagers who were impressed by the appearance of Clarke's clothes. They continued until they reached a large house where a woman of about 40 years old was, dark-skinned with a vibrant head of curly black hair. She wore giant glasses that protected her from a welding job she was doing on some pipes.

—Hello Marcela, it's good to see you, you haven't lost your touch with your welder— Rex said in a jovial way.

— What do you want, Rex? What poor soul did you torment with your stories until you came back here?

—I didn't torment any, rather I saved one, and he's here— Rex said excitedly as he pointed to Clarke who was swallowing his pride, all embarrassed.
Marcela took off her glasses, turned off the welder, and looked up at Rex and then at Clarke.— Oh my God! But where did you get this Rex? This man looks like he's been swallowed by a Snorknork and spit back out. Besides, what are those clothes?

—Well, I don't know what a Snorknork is, but I understand that the problems of the journey are reflected in my appearance. I apologize for my clothes, I was lost in the desert until Rex found me and brought me here hoping to resupply.

—I see, so what Rex was saying was true... and where do you come from? What's your name?

—My name is Clarke — followed by this, he told her his story and how he had arrived in this world.

Marcela looked at him doubtfully but replied— You're lucky that Rex found you and brought you to me first. Very few people would believe a story like that, but I could say that I've seen things that are extraordinary. And well, someone capable enough to withstand a journey in the desert with Rex deserves the opportunity to be helped. So let me offer you some things to get you settled and then we'll talk about how you'll pay me.

Clarke nodded and thanked Marcela and Rex for their help. He watched as she got him some clothes in that house that looked like a workshop, with pipes everywhere and tools. She showed him where the bathroom was and offered him food and water.

Hours passed and Clarke had already recovered. He had clothes suitable for the place, he was fed and refreshed. He felt very good. He had been observing this strange house/workshop and how things worked. He realized that the water came from underground wells extracted by large pumps that distributed it throughout the village. These pumps worked with a very different electricity and did not resemble anything he had seen before. It came from magical crystals that were enclosed in machines like ovens and the kinetic heat expelled from them was transformed into energy that allowed lights and machines to be turned on. All this seemed extremely fascinating to him.

He continued observing all the strange things about the house and the village, like the kuras which were in fact a creature related to turtles, but mixed with a beaver, since its tail, head, and legs were very similar to the latter, but it possessed a large shell.

Night fell, and Clarke was in the house/workshop where Marcela invited him to sit at the table to eat with her, Rex, and a little girl about 8 years old.

—Welcome, Clarke, now you look much more normal and better than when I saw you a few hours ago — said Marcela, serving herself a plate of meat and passing a bowl of salad with pieces of cactus.— By the way, this is my daughter Saraí, she's already learning all kinds of pipe welding.

—Hello Saraí, nice to meet you. Thank you Marcela for all your help, I really haven't felt this good in a long time, and wow, she's so young and already working with welding and metals? - said Clarke as he received the bowl and passed it.

— Well, of course, I've been training her since she was 5. What else could she be doing?

Clarke was impressed by the fact that such a young girl was not in school and was doing such a hard, heavy, and dangerous job as welding, but he quickly intuited that this could be something normal in this world and said.— No, nothing. The truth is that I was surprised because I also do welding, but I didn't start so young. By the way, where are the air conditioners? In this desert it's very hot and I don't see how you cool your homes, it feels quite cool in here.

—Air conditioners? What's that? — Marcela asked, confused.

—The Air conditioners are machines that cool or heat homes and make them reach very comfortable temperatures; in the place where I come from every house has one.

Marcela, Rex, and Saraí just stared at him. They had no idea what he was talking about.

Rex laughed and said — See why I brought him here, Marcela? Clarke always tells those weird tales of machines and things that nobody understands. He's someone with a lot of imagination.

— It's not an invention of mine, the truth is that it's something very common where I come from and it's strange not to see how you cool these houses, but it feels very cool for the extreme heat that's out there — said Clarke trying to clarify that he wasn't crazy and that he was speaking the truth.

— You have all kinds of stories, Clarke, very strange, but I believe you. However, I can tell you that we don't have anything like what you're saying. We all withstand the scorching heat of Zal with the magic crystals that are extracted from the mines near here — said Marcela and then she took a blue crystal that she had on a piece of furniture and broke it. This crystal emitted a magical air that impregnated her and the entire interior of the house.

Clarke felt a cold wind that stayed on his body and noticed how the temperature of the place decreased until it even got a little cold. He was impressed.

—Well, it was time to use a new crystal, it was the right time to do it and show you your answer of how the people of Zal withstand this scorching heat of the two suns — said Marcela. –The truth is that, without these crystals, the habitants of Zal could not live.

Clarke could not believe it and his face could not contain the expression of surprise.

— It seems that you have not seen the magic crystals, nor their magic nor anything like that, I don't know where you come from Clarke, but if you are interested, you still owe me the favor for the lodging and the help that I gave you. You could work tomorrow with the master miner

Duspathalyn for the crystal mines and learn more about them. What do you think?

—That sounds good to me, and I'm glad to be able to pay off my debt to you that way — Clarke knew that hard work wasn't going to be an impediment and with his health the way it was, he felt it would be perfect, plus he had a great interest in these crystals and how they worked. Besides, he hadn't forgotten Dr. Lee's challenge to help and give to others. So, it seemed like a good starting point.

—Perfect, Clarke, I'll let Duspathalyn know that you're starting with him tomorrow, just don't take it personally how he does things.

Everyone got up from the table, and Clarke helped to clean the plates. He spent a little more time with Marcela, Saraí, and Rex and then went to the hut where they had offered him a place to sleep. When he arrived, he realized it was a tool and junk storage room where Rex also slept on the floor on a rug.

—No way, this must be a joke! — said Clarke, disgusted by the space and the company.

—Hey Clarke, I was waiting for you to sleep, I saved you a spot here next to me. Besides, I was waiting for one of your stories to fall asleep— Rex said cheerfully, wagging his tail.

—There are no stories, just silence and sleep— Clarke said with annoyance and resigning himself to sleeping on the floor.

Don't be mean, Clarke, tell a short story. Or... I know! I'll start, I have a story for you were once I was in a Kura race and mine was the fastest, I felt the wind moving my cheeks from the great speed I was going and...— Rex recounted excitedly as Clarke placed a cushion over his head and looked for an escape from sleep to avoid finishing listening to another of Rex's stories.

Soon, Clarke's eyes started to feel heavy, and he drifted off to sleep.

Chapter 6: The Mine of Magic Crystals

It was early in the morning when Clarke awoke from a rather unpleasant night on the rug of that small hut, where he had slept next to Rex who was restless and noisy. Clarke opened his eyes and realized that his dog/hyena friend was gone and he could already hear activity in the village outside. He got up, shook off the sand that had been stirred up by the night's breezes, and washed his face with a water basin that was nearby, as in all the houses and huts of the village of Zira

As he went outside, the radiant glow of Zal's two suns struck his face and blinded him. Once again, he found himself facing the scorching heat of the desert.

Suddenly, he heard a familiar female voice — Good morning Clarke, I'm glad I didn't have to come wake you up. The team is getting ready to head out to the mines.

Clarke turned around and realized it was Marcela, who had a look of satisfaction on her face.

— Good morning Marcela, you don't have to worry about that, I'm used to getting up early. Where I come from, I've spent most of my life getting up early to be ready for work — he replied sincerely

—Well, I'm glad to hear that, let's not waste any time and let me introduce you to Duspathalyn. He's in charge of the work in the mines. He's around here somewhere.

— All right, I'll follow you— Clarke replied.

They walked through the village and approached a dwarven man with a bushy beard and a jug of what appeared to be beer. He was directing the workers as they loaded all the tools onto the Kuras, preparing to head for the mines.

—Come on, you lazy bums, I don't have all day for this, move it or I'll feed you to some Snorknorks.— Duspathalyn yelled while gulping down more of his jug.

—Excuse me, Mr. Duspathalyn, I've brought you a new worker.— Marcela said respectfully.

—Hello Mr. Duspathalyn, my name is Clarke, it's a pleasure to meet you — Clarke said, extending his hand for a formal greeting.

Duspathalyn looked at him strangely and said— And who's this? Where did you find him, Marcela? He doesn't look like he's from around here — After saying this, he took another swig of his beer without returning Clarke's greeting.

—He's come from far away, but he's fit for work and he also owes me a favor, so it's two birds down with one shot.

—Don't worry Mr. Duspathalyn, you'll see I can do a good job — Clarke said confidently.

—We'll see about that— Duspathalyn replied dryly as he gestured for Clarke to help the others load the Kuras.

With all the picks, shovels, and other tools loaded onto these giant turtle mounts called Kuras, the entire group set off for the mines. The journey was not short, and the heat of the two suns didn't make it pleasant. Clarke watched as everyone had small fragments of blue crystal that they would break from time to time to cool off, something that provided great relief. But at the same time, Clarke realized that while doing so, part of that cold gas it released wasn't cold at all and generated a cloud of gas that rose into the atmosphere.

He also noticed how anything that was impregnated with that gas was not only experiencing a decrease in temperature but also looked like the area near the fragmentation was deteriorating, the clothes were fading, the hands of whoever broke them were cracking, and the shell of the Kuras was losing its shine. It seemed that the crystal consumed part of the vitality of its surroundings, but it wasn't clear, since the marks disappeared within minutes.

After a while and a long journey, Clarke could see in the distance the magical crystal mines of Zal. It was a rock formation that gave way to a cave that plunged into the depths of the desert. There, other workers were breaking the rocks looking for such precious and necessary crystal.

— Alright, it's time to wake up —Duspathalyn shouted, making sure all his workers started quickly. —You've rested enough on the journey, and now it's time to work properly. Grab your shovels, picks, and hammers and let's get started because there's a lot of competition for those crystals today. No slacking off! —

Everyone grabbed their tools and walked in a line towards the rocky cave. Duspathalyn saw

Clarke and said,— Hey you, newbie. Don't lag behind and follow the rest—he said as he headed towards other dwarves who were in charge of the mine work and the groups of miners.

The rock formation was arid and vast, everything seemed full of rocks and sand with no crystals at the entrance, until you ventured into the deepest caverns and there you began to hear more frequently and loudly the constant hammering of iron tools hitting the rocks in search of the precious crystal.

Clarke observed the cave and although he had never worked as a miner, he knew that the goal was to find a vein of the mineral and extract it to get the crystal from there. However, observing all the other workers, he realized that getting a crystal was not easy at all.

The miners constantly demolished several tons of rock until they even got some crystal. If they got any, they usually started fighting over it, especially if it was blue, which was the crystal that was most used to cool off and lower the temperatures of whoever broke it, something that could save someone's life, even if only for a while if they were exposed to the heat of the suns.

Clarke was astonished. Given the rate at which people used it, he thought this crystal was much more common and easier to obtain. The truth was that it required a lot of effort, and he couldn't help but wonder in his head: How long will this be sustainable?

—Hey rookie! Don't just stand there, start chipping away at the rock— said one of the miners working on Clarke's team.

Clarke began to shovel and hammer at the rocks, hoping to find crystals and do a good job. His pride wouldn't allow him to do a bad job, even though he wasn't properly trained.

He hit the rocks with force, loaded and moved heavy stones, and sweated more than he had in a long time while working. His hands started to get calloused, and he could feel his muscles burning from the exertion. There was no human resources department here, nor any consideration for the miner. Without knowing it, he had volunteered for what he considered to be slave labor.

To make things even harder, Duspathalyn would constantly walk around yelling and scolding the miners while drinking a large jug of beer. — Come on, you useless! I haven't seen enough crystals today. Nobody's leaving here until I see results— he would say with authority and a bit of a drunken slur.

Clarke noticed how the miners respected Duspathalyn's authority when he was present, but when his back was turned, he saw how they hated and loathed him with gestures and words. Every time they heard the heavy footsteps of Duspathalyn's boots, they would all mutter about him with annoyance.

Clarke couldn't help but have flashbacks to his time as a manager, and how Duspathalyn was a similar reflection (albeit a bit more extreme) of his own attitudes as a manager. He was realizing how, instead of helping the team, he was making them feel worse and making the work harder. How his mere presence and that tyrannical attitude, instead of motivating, was dragging morale to the ground.

He repeated to himself that he would no longer be that person and that he shouldn't tolerate that treatment anymore. So, if what he needed to get out of this cave was to find a crystal, he was going to do it so he could never come back.

Clarke hit the rocks with a lot of energy, hitting and hitting, driven by his own rage at having become a tyrant and not the leader he dreamed of being. He hit and hit, feeling how each blow was molding something inside himself to stop being that figure that so many detested and that he now recognized. He hit, kicking up debris and surprising his companions who looked at him as if he had entered a trance. He hit and hit for hours, with one thing in mind: to get out of there and never return. His pride pushed him not to give up and to be better than he was before entering these mines. He kept hitting despite the fatigue, and when he was about to stop, he convinced himself a little more by saying, —Just a few more hits, Clarke, don't give up! — He used this technique several times until, in a flash of one of his pickaxes blows, a large blue crystal appeared between the rocks.

Such was Clarke's excitement that he shouted without thinking—Here! I found a blue crystal here!— he yelled excitedly and as an involuntary reaction to the pleasant surprise of having found a large crystal when he already felt he couldn't go on.

At that moment, Clarke's companions looked at him with astonishment, but at the same time with concern, as the miners from other groups had also heard him and it seemed they were going to pounce on him.

Clarke noticed his carelessness and observed all the miners around him who didn't work for Duspathalyn and who wanted that crystal for themselves. They had also been mining all day or even longer and were looking for their ticket out.

Time seemed to slow down, and Clarke could see how in a matter of seconds, complete chaos unfolded. All the miners in his area raised their picks, hammers, and shovels to fight to the death for the coveted crystal. Clarke, with his pick in hand, knew he had to protect himself, but he wasn't a warrior and his last fight was when he was a kid in school many decades ago.

His companions jumped to the rescue, and blows were exchanged from both sides. One guy managed to reach Clarke and swung a hammer at him, which he luckily managed to dodge by throwing himself to the side onto the floor.

Clarke crawled while trying to move away from the area and get to his feet. At that moment, another hammer blow was aimed at his head, but he managed to deflect it with the pick he was holding, putting it in front of him. However, his pick broke from the impact.

There was Clarke, on the floor, unarmed, looking up at a dark elf who was smiling at him with a perverted expression, raising the hammer to give him a final blow. —The crystal will be mine, you stupid human. Thanks for getting it for me, now take your prize!

Clarke closed his eyes and waited for the final blow at any moment. However, when he opened his eyes, he saw no dark elf. Beside him was Duspathalyn who, with a strong blow of his hammer, had sent the dark elf flying to the other end of the cave.

Instantly, other dwarves arrived and they all controlled the situation, making sure that all the miners returned to their posts.

— Clarke, I think you're lacking in brains. You made a big mess by shouting out loud about your find, but I must admit I haven't seen a blue crystal of that size in a long time. I'm sure we can get a lot of fragments from that crystal. Take it out and you can leave this cave. That will get you a month off work— said Duspathalyn calmly as he handed Clarke another pickaxe.

Clarke hit the rock and extracted the enormous crystal. To his surprise, behind it was another, smaller one. He carefully removed it and put it in his pocket. Clarke was very curious to understand crystals and wasn't going to waste the opportunity, even though he knew that no one should remove crystals without giving them to Duspathalyn, so he kept it a secret and with great care.

Clarke dropped his tools and went to Duspathalyn, who took the enormous crystal from him and congratulated him. — Well done, Clarke, you turned out to be not as useless as most. You earned a toast with me while the first kura is prepared to return to the village— Duspathalyn finished saying as he handed a beer to Clarke, patted him on the back, and drank the entire jug of beer from his hand. —Ah... back to work with the other useless ones. Well, such is the hard life of a Dwarf— said Duspathalyn as he bid farewell to Clarke and walked back into the depths of the cave. Clarke discreetly threw away the hot beer that Duspathalyn had given him and thought about how crazy someone had to be to drink that in such scorching heat.

The next urka leaving for the village of Zira was ready after waiting for an hour. Clarke got on board with a group of miners on their way back. Clarke watched the horizon with a sunset of two prisms of colors intertwined in the center of the two suns above the sky of Zal. Today he almost died, again. He had learned many strange things about this world and was sure of one thing. He would do anything to never set foot in those mines again.

Chapter 7: Do Something Useful

The Urka was taking its final steps to reach the village of Zira. All the passengers got off with their belongings while another group of people tended to the animal.

Clarke got off a bit sore from all the physical exertion he had done in the mines. He was eager to talk to Marcela and settle his debt, making it clear that he wouldn't be touching the mines for another day.

When he arrived at the house where Marcela lived, he realized that neither she nor her daughter Saraí were there. However, he found a white-bearded dwarf who was stocking the warehouse with crystals. This dwarf, upon seeing Clarke, said— If you're looking for Marcela, she left a while ago. She should be arriving soon. I can see by your looks that you've just arrived from the mines, haven't you?

—Yes, I just arrived with a group of miners who were lucky enough to find some crystals—said Clarke while cooling off a bit inside the house that had the effect of a magical crystal that was still active.

— It's true, you're very lucky if you were only in the mines for a day. It wasn't like that before, but now it seems like there are fewer and fewer crystals. Miners can spend weeks looking for one, and the truth is that people in this village and other corners of the desert need them more and more.

— You're right, I've noticed that the heat here is unbearable and that the crystals help, but the fact that over time their effect wears off and the crystal is no longer useful is like a waste. Besides, I think the crystal consumes some of the vitality of its surroundings when it releases its magical gas.

The dwarf raised an eyebrow and stopped what he was doing to address Clarke. —That's curious. Very few people pay attention to that detail. They're usually so focused on using them and reducing the suffocating heat that they overlook it or some even ignore it. But not you. What's your name?

— My name is Clarke, it's a pleasure to meet you. And what's your name?

—Pleased to meet you, I'm called Halsin, I'm one of the oldest suppliers of magical crystals in this village. They're very good people, but they don't see beyond the sphere —said Halsin as he turned to pick up his box of crystals.— I would like to continue talking to you, but people are waiting for their crystals. We'll be in touch, here, I'll leave you a badge, I'm bad with faces and names, but if you show it to me, I'll remember you and what we talked about. See you later— he handed a small metal badge in the shape of a pickaxe to Clarke and left the shop.

Clarke was curious about what Halsin might know about the crystals. He had the impression that they were more of a problem than a blessing, however, he knew that, in this world, living without their use and being exposed to such heat would be impossible for life as these people knew it. Perhaps they had something to do with what Dr. Lee was referring to. But Clarke still wasn't sure.

After a while, Clarke was still waiting at the reception of Marcela's house when Rex arrived with her and Saraí. Clarke approached them and greeted them. Marcela greeted him with a hug and said— Duspathalyn sent me a letter letting me know what you got in the cave, no doubt that will be of great help to the village. Good job.

— Uh, thanks, I guess. You never told me that my life would be at risk working there or that I wouldn't get out of the mines without getting some crystal. That would have been good to know— said Clarke, showing a touch of annoyance.

—And what did you expect? To work on something easier like bathing the kuras? Clarke, I know you're new. But here in the village of Zira, everyone contributes something that is considered of equal value to the community. Some go to the mines, others work as guards, but those are skilled warriors — referring to the fact that just by appearance, she knew Clarke didn't know how to fight —others take care of the kuras, which are usually anxious, and so everyone contributes something. I thought the mines would help you pay for your lodging, food, and stay. The truth is, you did a good job — said Marcela sincerely—You don't have to go back there if you don't want to, but you have to find something that the community accepts as of equal value or you'll lose the right to be here — she said more seriously.

Clarke was surprised by how things worked in the village and what his options might be. Then he said —Okay Marcela, Duspathalyn also told me that my find would be equivalent to a month's work; I guess I have until then to figure out what I should do.

Marcela nodded in approval, as she prepared dinner for everyone to eat since night was falling. Clarke joined them and with nightfall, after dinner, he went back to the storage hut where he slept with Rex.

Lying on the rug and looking at the ceiling, Clarke asked aloud —Hey Rex, if we all collaborate in the village, what is your job?

Rex wagged his tail and said — I'm glad you asked, Clarke. I roam the dunes of the Zal desert, securing the perimeter and often coming across travelers, wanderers, and strangers like you, to guide them to the village and find new people to help.

—And how common is it for you to find people like me?

— Hmmm... well, truth be told, you're the first one like you. The outskirts of Zira tend to be very sparsely populated with friendly creatures. So I usually spend my days alone with the desert until I saw you.

Clarke, doubting the relevance of Rex's work, asked him— How many individuals work as searchers, like you?

—Hmmm... I hadn't thought about it, but I think I'm the only one. Well, there are other Sharq like me, but they do other more specific searches for Marcela— said Rex with an innocent smile.

Clarke realized that it wasn't a job option he could do, possibly that was just a job invented to keep Rex out of the village and thus avoid listening to his incessant chatter.

Clarke settled on the rug to sleep and wished Rex good night, who returned the sentiment and settled down beside him, beginning to tell a story of how Rex one day wandering through the desert saw mirages and thought that suddenly the sky had three suns.

Lost in thought, Clarke examined the crystal in detail, holding it in his hand. He could see how through its blue crystal, there was this magical gas that mixed with a liquid. Something about that crystal caught his attention, but he couldn't quite put his finger on what it was. He closed his eyes and soon fell asleep.

The next day, with the first glimmer of the two suns, Clarke woke up and, as usual, Rex had already started his journey to patrol the outskirts looking for new people. Clarke got up, washed his face, and went for a walk around the village.

He found a big house where they were serving breakfast, and as was customary in the village, if your work quota was met, you were welcome to receive your portion. Clarke took a plate and sat at a table that had a view of the entire place. There he saw how individuals, couples, and families gathered to eat. Everyone at that moment seemed very cordial.

Among the many things he observed, he noticed how at one table, a small child began to sweat a lot and the mother handed him a small piece of blue crystal to break. At that moment, Clarke looked closely and saw that when the child broke it, the magical gas of the crystal was released and it permeated the child, giving him relief and lowering his temperature. But at the same time, his hands, which broke the crystal, not only lost a little of their shine but also left a burn mark, a frostbite burn.

At that moment, Clarke had a flashback; of when he was an air conditioning apprentice and practiced placing the gauges on the air conditioning machine. At that time, he had no experience and made the mistake of being very nervous and not tightening the hoses properly, which caused some refrigerant gas to escape and hit his hand, leaving a small frostbite burn.

Clarke came to his senses, and realized, he became conscious of that strange feeling of familiarity that came from seeing the blue crystals. They reminded him of the refrigerant gas contained in a container and how, despite being magical and different, it maintained many similarities.

Clarke found it curious, but he still had more questions. He needed to find Halsin who seemed to know more about it. Clarke finished eating and got up from his table, decided to visit Marcela to ask her about Halsin's whereabouts.

Once at Marcela's house, Clarke found her welding some pipes and, approaching her, said

— Hello Marcela, sorry to bother you, do you know where I can find Halsin?

— Hello Clarke, I'd like to tell you yes, but the dwarves are never still and are always busy with their affairs. Halsin is in charge of sending his people to deliver crystals to all this village and others; and even sometimes he makes the delivery in person himself. The truth is, it would be better if you wait for him, although if you ask me, you're wasting your time looking for a dwarf — said Marcela while stopping welding to answer.

— Oh, well, but in that case if I have the time, when do you think the next time he'll come?

—He usually comes to the village every 3 weeks or so, but he doesn't really have a schedule. Can I ask why you're looking for him?

—I have questions about his work, thanks Marcela. I'll keep that in mind. I'll leave you to continue with your things — said Clarke, as he quickly left the house.

Clarke didn't have time to sit and wait as he was clear that he didn't want to go back to the mines, which, if he had to go back, he might not be so lucky as to return quickly or to find Halsin. He needed to stay in the village or find him. Besides, he was still thinking about Dr. Lee's words about rebuilding his life by giving what he hadn't given to others in a year's time. He had to find a way to help the village and felt it had something to do with the extreme heat and the crystals.

Clarke left the house frustrated and walked through the village trying to find an answer to his problem. He observed that, among the available jobs, there was that of a cook, but the menu of this world was very different, he didn't usually cook even when he was in Florida; his home of origin, because his long workdays almost always left him without energy and he subsisted on fast food or for a while on what his wife made for him until they got divorced. Clarke never really cooked and now in this desert, with strange creatures and foods, it wasn't an option.

Clarke also observed other jobs that weren't even worth considering. He self-evaluated and knew that he didn't have the skills or the time to learn them. The job of a guard seemed very dangerous, because within the village there was an apparent order, but at night and in its surroundings there could be dangers like bandits or creatures that he would have to fight to the death and he was not a warrior and noticed how many people were accustomed to a hostile life with their experience in the mines and with the fire gnomes, after those memories he knew he was lucky to have been able to get out of those situations in one piece.

Clarke was running out of options, and the scorching heat wasn't helping him think clearly. He continued to walk through the village, looking for something useful he could work on, and looking at the horizon, at one end of the village. He saw a shadow in the distance and, looking at it more closely, saw that it was a Sharq with its nose raised. It was Rex and he was sniffing something. At that moment, Clarke clicked and a great idea came to his mind. What if Rex could smell Halsin? It would be perfect to find him quickly. He just had to ask him.

Clarke ran towards Rex, waving his hands with the intention of getting his attention and getting him to come closer, shouting— Hey Rex! Rex, come here!

At that moment Rex managed to hear him and immediately ran towards him.— Hello, Clarke, is something wrong?

—Yes, friend, I need a favor from you. Can you follow the scent of a specific person with your nose, even if they are far from the village?

—Yes, Clarke, that's my specialty, but who are you looking for? Who got lost?

—No one is lost, but I need to know where he is and talk to that person.

— Well, I need something of theirs to sniff and from there follow that trail to their position.

Clarke smiled and handed him the small emblem that Halsin had given him in their conversation when he met him at Marcela's house — I hope this works.

—Of course it will, this is perfect Clarke, I can follow the trail, but it's almost dusk and it would be dangerous if night falls on us in the desert.

—Do you think you could follow the trail tomorrow?

— Of course! As sure as my name is Rex and I have four legs... or are they two hands and two feet? Ahh! You understood me.

Clarke smiled, Rex might be a little annoying with his excessive chatter and absurd stories, but there was no doubt that he was very helpful and had helped him on more than one occasion. Once again, he was depending on him, and with his good sense of smell there was a chance of finding Halsin.

Clarke got excited and crouched down to pat Rex affectionately.

At that moment Rex froze and said — What are you doing, Clarke?

—Uhh... I'm patting you. Where I come from it means a gesture of appreciation that people give to the animals they appreciate. Really Rex, thank you very much for all your help — said Clarke as he stepped back and stood up.

— Oh well, if that's what it means, it's good to know. No one has ever thanked me like that before, so it's a pleasure to help you.

—How curious, I almost forget how to say thank you, Rex. But I promised someone I would remember how to do it and your help has served me for that and much more. So thank you again.

Rex smiled back at Clarke and they both walked back to the village. Both new friends felt a great joy for the gesture of sincere friendship and gratitude that had arisen. Rex felt happy to feel appreciated by someone when most of his life he had been made to feel like a nuisance and a great outcast. Clarke felt at peace, because he was learning to value others more and to leave behind the old and proud Clarke who didn't need anything or anyone. Although it still stung his pride that he was learning this from a dog and not a person. But he had to start somewhere.

Chapter 8: The Risky Quest

That morning, Clarke woke up early with Rex, who always went out at the first hint of sunlight as it peeked over Zal's sky. Clarke equipped with his desert attire, which helped him somewhat to endure the extreme heat: a pair of goggles to protect his eyes from the sand that the winds stirred up in the dunes, and a good canteen of water. However, he hoped the journey wouldn't be too long.

They left the village of Zira on foot, as they couldn't use one of the kura for their journey to find Halsin. The village only used their kura for things considered important to the community. Rex led the way and the walk, sniffing Halsin's emblem.

— Hey Rex, do you think you can follow this trail without getting confused?— Clarke asked.

—Of course! —Rex replied —The smell of dwarves is very distinctive. They're always drinking beer, and their things get soaked in that aroma.

—And aren't you going to get confused and sniff out anyone who is drinking that beer? — Clarke asked.

—Clarke, you're new around here. It's very rare to drink beer if you're not a dwarf. Most races in Zal fight dehydration and drink a lot of water, the dwarves don't suffer from that problem. So calm down.

Clarke admired how much Rex knew about the desert, his village, and their cultures. He seemed like a very wise companion and pleasant company. A feeling that lasted until Rex started telling a new story about how he once spent weeks following a trail that went in circles, until he realized he was following his own trail.

After hours of intense walking, Clarke was consuming the water from his canteen, already, because of the immense heat, his water had the temperature of a good hot coffee, but with the taste of water when it mixes with the sand.

—How much longer, Rex?— Clarke asked, sounding a bit exhausted.

— I don't know, Clarke. The smell usually intensifies when I'm closer to the subject or object. So, if we don't see anyone on the horizon, it must mean we still have a long way to go.

As they walked, Clarke put his hand in his pocket where he could feel his blue crystal, which he guarded jealously. He really wanted to use it to cool down and lower his temperature in the immense heat, but he also felt he shouldn't. This crystal could be useful later.

Clarke looked up at the sky and saw how those two bright suns radiated their full intensity on him, Rex, and the sands of the dunes. Sweat soaked his clothes, and the dry, arid desert wind dried them. Rex was much more accustomed to life in these extreme temperatures, but he needed to hydrate from time to time.

Both friends continued their journey with their willpower faltering with each step without a visible goal. However, at one point they stopped when they saw something that caught their attention.

That something was a cave, which had a rock formation that rose above the sands of the desert. It seemed that the cave went through part of the sea of dunes and could be a shady relief to avoid all the heat of the rays of the two suns.

Clarke immediately ran inside and Rex followed him. There, Clarke tried to take a sip from his canteen, but it was already empty. Rex observed Clarke who was already at a critical point and needed to drink something and told him — Clarke don't give up yet, surely in this cave there is water that we can find, I feel the humidity in the air.

Clarke was motivated and also recognized the humidity in the air, it gave him memories of the humidity he felt in the summers in Florida. Thus, both advanced through the cave, guided by their need to find water. The cave was dark and humid, was full of stalactites and stalagmites. From time to time, they saw flashes of light that came from some shiny stones embedded in the walls.

—Look at those stones. They look like diamonds — said Clarke, admiring the stones. —Rex, are they another type of magic crystals?

—Yes, Clarke, those are the electric crystals that Marcela uses to weld the pipes and thus supply the whole village with their power. They're beautiful. But they're also dangerous. Don't you see that they're electrified? If you touch them, they'll give you a shock— Rex warned, avoiding the stones.

—Don't be so dramatic, Rex. Besides, they're wet and it would be perfect to be able to get water out of them. I don't think they're that dangerous. Look, I'm going to touch one…— said Clarke, reaching out to a stone.

—No, Clarke! Don't do it! It's crazy!— shouted Rex, trying to stop Clarke.

Clarke remembered the last time he didn't listen to Rex and how he had never shown him anything that wasn't sincere, so he decided to listen to him this time.

—Okay Rex, thanks for the information. Let's keep looking for where to get water carefully. I think I hear a stream of water ahead.

— Yes, I can smell it too— Rex affirmed with enthusiasm.

The two friends continued their steps through the cave, avoiding any contact with the crystals and getting closer and closer to the stream of water. Its sound grew louder and louder, but there was no visual trace of it.

With each step forward and deeper into the cave, the sound became louder and louder, indicating that they were approaching its origin. But it also became louder, indicating that there was something more than water.

—Rex, what's that noise?— Clarke asked, worried.

—I don't know, Clarke. It sounds like the sound of a waterfall. Or a cataract. Or...— said Rex, interrupting himself upon seeing what was in front of them.

—Rushing water! — exclaimed Clarke, terrified.

Clarke and Rex found themselves facing a huge mass of water coming out of one end of the cave, forming a river that ran along the ground. The water was crystal clear and reflected the light of the stones. But it was also violent and dragged everything it found in its path.

—There it comes! — said Rex, horrified.

—Rex, hold on to me! —said Clarke, as he climbed onto some nearby rocks.

Unable to escape the unexpected torrent of water, Clarke and Rex held on as best they could, with all their strength, to a rock column at one end of the cave walls. The water rapidly approached with a huge torrent as if a water tap had been turned on under a lot of pressure, and in a matter of seconds it hit the two friends.

—¡Aaaah! — screamed Clarke and Rex, feeling the water pushing and carrying them away.

Clarke and Rex were dragged by the water, unable to resist. The water submerged them and pulled them back up to the surface. The water hit them and shook them violently. It made them feel cold and a tingling sensation. It carried them from one end of the cave to the other.

—Clarke, I'm wet!— Rex yelled, being obvious.

—Rex, don't let go of me, friend! — Clarke said, lifting his head above the water to keep an eye on him.

—Clarke, I'm scared! — Rex said, sincerely.

—Rex, take my hand! — Clarke yelled, reaching out his hand to Rex.

They continued to be dragged by the water, unable to control their fate. Clarke made a huge effort to avoid the rocks as he was dragged along and to help his friend who was having great difficulty staying afloat.

In one of those sudden movements of the water, Clarke noticed how Rex was pushed towards a rock and hit his head, leaving him apparently unconscious as he no longer moved and his body was directed like a rag doll by the waters.

Determined not to lose his savior and only friend, Clarke used all the strength that adrenaline could give him in such a stressful situation and swam with all his might towards him. Clarke took him in his arms and, lucky to have a tunnel inside the cave that led to calmer waters, he went inside until he found a space to catch his breath. There, with his friend in his arms, he managed to climb onto a rock and get half his body out of the water. Clarke knew first aid, but for humans, never for animals, so he didn't know exactly what to do with Rex who wasn't responding.

—Come on Rex, wake up! Don't leave me alone in this, friend... you have to wake up— Clarke said desperately, unable to accept losing Rex in this way, much less when it was his idea to go into the cave. He shook Rex's body, but it didn't move. His eyes were white and his snout was slack.

Clarke began to shed tears against his will, as he stood soaked and carrying his friend's body, alone in the quiet, dark cave — Don't leave me Rex! Please, friend, I haven't had the chance to call anyone a friend in a long time, not in this world or where I came from. I haven't given myself the opportunity to meet and trust people or animals, and in the few times I did, I didn't give them the time they deserved. I don't want to be left without friends again, Rex... please wake up — Clarke cried as he hugged Rex's body.

Suddenly, in the middle of that big hug, Clarke heard —¡Caugh! Caugh! Clarke, that's so sweet, no one has ever said such lovely words to me. You should say them more often, you know? — Rex said waking up.

—Rex! You're alive! I thought you were dead— said Clarke joyfully.

— Sorry Clarke, I forgot to tell you that I tend to instinctively go into a state of playing dead when I get hit or am in great danger. But I'm fine. And what's wrong with you? Were you crying?

—No, no, of course not... it's just all the water splashing in my face — Clarke said, trying to hide it as he wiped away the tears from his eyes.

—Well, that was a very sweet moment, Clarke, and I appreciate knowing that someone cares about me. I've never felt that in the village. But... I hate being wet and the fact that you're carrying me makes it even more uncomfortable. We need to get out of here.

—You're right, but the whole cave is full of water. I was really lucky to find this pocket of air, Rex. I don't know exactly where we are.

—It's curious, I've heard of the underwater currents that exist beneath the Zal desert, but I've never been in one. I don't know where to go either.

Faced with uncertainty, the two friends decided to wait and see if the water would recede. It seemed the current had stopped and, given the vastness of the cave and the fact that they were in a desert, the water should drain into the sand or evaporate quickly.

A couple of hours passed and Clarke and Rex were very cold. The darkness of the cave and the stagnant water that soaked their bodies had lowered their temperature. There was no sign of the water receding, in fact, it was starting to rise.

—Rex, we have a problem buddy.

—Oh no Clarke, the water is rising— said Rex, very scared.

—I know, we're going to have to swim back through the tunnel in the cave and find a way out— said Clarke, knowing they were between a rock and a hard place. There was no other choice.

They both agreed and took one last big breath of air until the cave they were in was completely covered in water. Clarke began to swim and behind him was Rex, who wasn't a very good swimmer.

They emerged from the submerged tunnel, following the lights coming from the crystals that illuminated the entire cave. Clarke noticed Rex's difficulty swimming and motioned for him to grab onto him. In this way, they both kicked their way through the cave, searching for any sign of a space to breathe or an exit.

Neither of them was willing to give up, and they were exerting their greatest physical and mental effort to persevere. Clarke never thought that after being so thirsty and eager to find water when he was in the desert, he would now reject it and fear it so much. With each stroke, he felt his need for air increase so much that his throat burned. Then, he noticed that at one point his friend Rex stopped kicking, and with one hand he decided to grab him while continuing to swim.

Suddenly, a glimmer of hope emerged from the cave ceiling; it was a crumbling hole that led to a space to escape the water. Clarke was elated, and with the little air he had left, he swam as fast as he could towards it. But he quickly felt each kick and stroke becoming more difficult, as if his body was getting heavier and instead of moving forward, he seemed to be sinking. Clarke saw his vision darken and as he reached out his hand to get out of the water, he lost consciousness. His body couldn't take it anymore..

Chapter 9: A Miraculous Idea

—He must be a crazy lost guy and his sharq — said a deep, masculine voice.

—That's why I always say, 'Never go into a cave without a dwarf' — a second, rough masculine voice replied.

—But are they alive?— the first voice asked.

—Looks like they're both starting to breathe, they just finished puking up all the water they swallowed— the second voice clarified.

Clarke opened his eyes at that moment with a blurry vision. He woke up disoriented, unable to contain a wet cough as he expelled jets of water.

— Welcome back to the world of the living, you lucky bastards— said the first voice.

— Easy, easy... let them recover first— said the second voice.

Clarke started to see better and focused his gaze on Rex, who was coughing up all the water he had swallowed. He looked up and saw two bearded dwarves who seemed to have rescued him.

— Can you hear us now? Can you understand us?— said Dwarf 1.

Clarke nodded affirmatively as he regained his speech.

— Perfect, you're lucky, friend. My brother and I were digging in the mines when we saw you through this hole we had just opened in the ground. And we found you. What are two non-dwarves doing wandering alone in the mines?— said Dwarf 1.

—We were... cough! cough!... looking for a dwarf named Halsin— Clarke said, still coughing.

Dwarf 2 raised an eyebrow with a look of interest — What's a human and a Sharq doing looking for Halsin in the desert?

—I have questions, that's all — Clarke replied, more composed.— He gave me this emblem with which I hoped to find him — Clarke pulled the emblem he still had from Halsin out of his pocket and showed it.

—That emblem is indeed Halsin's, how curious. What's your name, human?— said Dwarf 2.

—My name is Clarke, and yours?

—My name is Helmir and my brother's Björn. You're very lucky, Halsin is a good friend of ours and we know where he is. If what you want to talk to him about is so important, we won't have a problem taking you to him as he's at a nearby stop. Besides, when we saved you, we saw that you had something of our interest in your pockets.

Clarke realized something was missing. He checked his pockets and realized that they had taken the blue crystal he had been keeping. —I appreciate your help, but you could have just asked for it. – Clarke said, a little annoyed.

—You know that no crystal leaves the mines unless it's from a dwarf's hands. Something tells me you didn't get it legally. So, until we're with Halsin and he proves to me that you're trustworthy, this crystal will be mine — Helmir said.

Clarke shrugged and accepted Helmir's terms. After all, they had saved his and Rex's lives, and besides, they would take him to Halsin.

The group, now ready, began the march to leave the cave, where the two dwarf brothers knew perfectly well where to go. Rex followed behind, shaking the water out of his ears, and Clarke wondered with immense doubt if what he would learn from Halsin would be worth all that they had gone through. He didn't want to have anything else to regret.

After a while, they found themselves outside the cave, apparently in a different area from where Clarke and Rex had entered. There, a kura belonging to the two dwarf brothers was waiting for them, in which they all boarded and headed towards Halsin's location.

The journey across the dunes on top of the kura was no longer so heavy. However, it was impossible for Clarke not to feel bad about the suffocating heat of the Zal desert. Quickly, his abhorrence of all that water that had almost drowned him, turned into a longing for Clarke's throat that, in a crazy thought, wished he could have taken a little more of that water before leaving.

Within a few hours, the group arrived at a large village. This village had a much sturdier infrastructure than Zira's village and was almost becoming a small city. Its houses were made of well-crafted, wide, and low rocks. Clarke realized that this place was very different from the other village. Here, he noticed that dwarves predominated and there was a great abundance of crystals. There was a guard on every corner, heavily armed, and the atmosphere was one of order and authority.

— We have arrived, welcome to the imposing village of Hardwind. Surely your eyes have never seen anything like it— said Björn with a very proud voice.

— Here you can find Halsin, just follow this path to a two-story house with a crystal dome — said Helmir pointing to a path inside the village.

This village was so organized that all its paths seemed to be distributed in perfect grids between each building.

Clarke got off the kura, following Helmir's directions with his eyes. He said— Thank you, Helmir. I'll head that way. Are you coming later?

— Nah, I have other things to do here in the village, but I'll be in touch. I'll see you soon, Clarke — said Helmir as he began to ride away on the kura.

—Wow, Clarke, I've never seen a village like this in my life. What order — said Rex, surprised.

— It's true, it's a nice change from the other desert landscapes — said Clarke, noticing the difference between the places he had known in the Zal desert, but not surprised, as none of these villages compared to the structures of cities like New York or even downtown Orlando.

—Alright Rex, let's find Halsin— Clarke said, stepping into the village.

The two friends walked, their eyes darting from side to side. There were many crystals placed in the windows of some houses. The guards patrolled on a kind of dinosaur that resembled a velociraptor, with lizard skin but a tail covered in a lot of hair. It had four very strong legs. Clarke could only think that it looked like a strange mix between a lion and a dinosaur, used as a horse. They were covered in shiny and bright armor.

Rex saw the fascination in Clarke's eyes as he stared at the creatures. – Those are Zaripus – He explained –They're the fastest things in the Zal desert. A status symbol, really. –

They both continued walking, noticing that even exposed to the elements, the air didn't feel so hot. There were many cloth roofs that covered the spaces between the buildings and that were located very high, giving a little relief and shade to those who traveled in the village. But the blue crystals that were used everywhere in the place also did so. The Village was quite full of people and almost unanimously of Dwarves.

Clarke and Rex continued their way until they found Halsin's house. This house was a little taller than the others and had a strange crystal dome.

Clarke knocked on the door, but there was no answer. He opened it and peered inside the house. He entered before Rex and could see how there were hundreds of blue crystals in boxes and many plans and drawings about the two suns, space, and the constellations. In there, there was an air of knowledge and learning. There were large bookshelves and many books. Clarke looked on in wonder; he wasn't a habitual reader, but he appreciated seeing such a personal library in a house.

The silence was interrupted when Rex entered and began to call out for Halsin loudly - Halsin, Halsin, we're looking for you, we're from the village of Zira.

Clarke raised his hand to Rex with a gesture for him to be silent, and more respectfully said — Excuse me, Mr. Halsin, I've been looking for you since the Village of Zira! I'm Clarke, you gave me your emblem.

Just then, heavy footsteps with the sound of buckled boots came down and approached from some stairs. It was Halsin who was heading towards Clarke — I see, you're the human who had noticed the nature of the blue crystals, Clarke, if I remember correctly.

— Yes, that's right. I have questions about the crystals. Their nature and how they are used intrigue me, but I think their use is also partly a problem— said Clarke, unable to hide how much he was interested in the subject.

Halsin stroked his beard and with a curious gesture said— Hmmm, your guesses and your curiosity are not bad, but it would be better to talk about this on the second floor. We may be alone, but when the subject of crystals comes up, suddenly all ears are listening. In these matters, there can always be people who are offended by what we say — Halsin turned around and invited Rex and Clarke to go up the stairs.

In this second floor there was a section exposed to a crystal dome where a large telescope was located. It was a large study room and it maintained a more hermetic sound that distanced it from the outside sound. In this room you could observe blackboards with writings of what seemed to be mathematical formulas in another language and many prints about the crystals and the constellations.

Halsin sat on a chair, invited Clarke and Rex to do the same and took a jug of beer that he had left on a table. He took a sip until he emptied it and when he was about to refill it with a barrel that he had nearby he offered Rex and Clarke — Do you want a hot beer?

—No, thank you. We're fine with water— replied Clarke, not understanding how someone could drink hot beer with so much heat outside in the desert.

—Ah well, more for me!— replied Halsin, taking another swig. Then he continued —The truth, Clarke, is that magic crystals have been a relief and a necessity for the habitants of the great Zal desert for many years. Although some legends say that it was not always so, but these have almost been forgotten and today it is almost impossible to imagine a life without them. Some would even refuse. Because, as you see, crystals have become a matter of power and wealth, whoever has the crystals has in their power many creatures that suffocate in the heat and will do anything to cool themselves with them — Halsin took another sip of beer while Clarke looked at him and listened attentively.

Halsin continued —What you saw happening with the crystals is true, every time they break and their essence is released, part of it remains as a gas in the atmosphere and if my calculations are not wrong, they are to blame for the atmosphere heating up a little more each day. Today, I no longer think that there is much difference in how much more the desert can continue to heat up. People cannot live without the crystal. However, it is not an infinite resource and we dwarves know that very well. There will come a time, which I fear we are already close to, and people will not have enough crystals to meet the demand. There will be wars and rebellions over, even if it's just one crystal. That will be a chaos that, as you can see, the dwarves are prepared to win. But, not all of us want to reach that point. Not all of us are so greedy or selfish as to want that to happen. That's why I wanted to talk to you, Clarke. I heard that you come from an area where it's not so hot and people live without crystals. I want to know where it is or what it is. Maybe it's the salvation that many people need before the time of chaos arrives. Tell me, Clarke — Halsin stopped talking as he waited for a response.

Clarke was impressed by everything behind the crystals and how, perhaps due to the fact of coming from outside, he had noticed that something murky was happening until Halsin's clarification. Clarke put his hands on his knees while remaining seated and said — I don't know how to explain it, Halsin, and don't take me for crazy. But I don't think I can tell you exactly where I come from, the truth is I don't think it's this same world or universe. I don't even know exactly how I got here, or how to go back. I'm sorry.

Halsin was drinking from his jug of beer at that moment, but upon hearing Clarke's words, he suddenly slammed it down on the table and said - Then, we're screwed. We're just wasting time with something inevitable.

—No, maybe something can be done. Even if it sounds crazy— Clarke said confidently.

—What do you have in mind, Clarke? Unless it's otherworldly magic, I think several people, including myself, have tried to find a solution without much success— Halsin replied without much hope.

— It's not magic, but it's something that's very common in my world. I've seen that the electricity they use comes from electric crystals and that these never need to be broken or consumed for use. I know it as clean energy that doesn't harm the environment.

—Okay, but what do we do with that? We already use that energy everywhere and it doesn't present any solution — said Halsin, unimpressed.

Clarke continued — Well, with that same energy, I could create a machine that would work using the blue crystals as a compound to cool a specific area, in this case, I'm referring to the interiors of houses and buildings. It would practically be the same principle of conservation of energy. Using them without breaking them.

— It's useless, the crystal doesn't transfer its magic unless it's broken and once the crystal is broken, the liquid inside the crystal evaporates and if you try to contain it, the container freezes creating a large ball of ice that soon melts and loses the effect unless you break the container again and each time it loses more and more of its effect— said Halsin, looking discouraged.

Clarke continued — Yes, I figured that out. But for that, the crystal compound would be introduced into a hermetic system connected to a compressor that would displace the gas from the crystal and cause it to change from a gaseous state to a liquid state, and with the help of fans, they would generate the transfer of heat and cold. The same magical gas would undergo another change of state...

Halsin interrupted, standing up excitedly — I'm not sure I understand correctly. Are you telling me that this change of state would allow the compound to reach different temperatures and thus transfer its energy to change the temperature of a nearby area and cool it or, on the contrary, heat it? That's brilliant, Clarke. But how can that be done?

Clarke confidently replied — Halsin, we can thank the laws of thermodynamics for that. They explain how energy and temperature behave. For instance, they tell us that heat moves from a hotter object to a colder one. By using a compressor to pressurize this magical gas, causing it to change from a gas to a liquid and then back to a gas, we can exploit these phase changes to transfer heat.

— Are you saying we could build a machine that would hermetically seal this blue crystal compound and change its state, allowing it to transfer heat or cold depending on the environment? That's incredible, Clarke — Halsin exclaimed.

— Yes, in principle. But it's just a theory. I don't know if the crystal compound is like any of the refrigerants we use in my world, and I'm not an engineer. I used to repair machines, not build them. But I think this could be a good solution for life in the villages. We could escape this heat and reduce our reliance on crystals. We would still need them, but we wouldn't have to destroy them, avoiding an imminent shortage — Clarke said.

—Yes, it could work, Clarke. I didn't know there were humans so intelligent... those who only live less than a hundred years —Halsin scratched his beard as he walked around the room and continued — This is huge, too big for everyone to know. We need to work on building this machine. I'll give you some blue crystals to fund you and for you to work with them. You'll have to build the machine in the village of Zira in secret, because here there may be people who don't like our idea and a human would attract a lot of attention. I'll be visiting you and several of my most trusted colleagues. We'll build that machine, Clarke! — Said Halsin, grabbing his jug of beer and giving Clarke a hug and a friendly shake to Rex. —Today we celebrate! friends, and tomorrow we leave in a kura for Zira with the plan in hand. Hahaha, the current history books will be rewritten with our names, friends! Cheers to that! — And Halsin proceeded to drink his entire jug of beer in one gulp.

Rex started to jump and wag his tail excitedly and Clarke began to feel a great joy. He had managed to materialize a plan to help people and, incidentally, not return to the mines. At that moment, Clarke felt a warm memory of Doctor Lee and his message about having to become a better person and contribute something great to others in order to have a new opportunity to return. He felt that this was the right direction to return to his world and do good. He didn't know what challenges he would face during construction, but he was willing to try and to count on this new team of people and creatures to manage to build it before completing a year in that desert.

Chapter 10: Let's Get to Work

After an emotional night of philosophical, physical, and mathematical discussions, Clarke and Rex had risen early, having spent the night at Halsin's home. Together with him, they were preparing to equip and have ready a kura that would take them, the plan, and some of the materials from the dwarven village of Hardwind to their more modest trading village of Zira.

— Alright lads, the kura is now equipped with the crystals, various tools, and equipment for you to start working on the machine. I'll see you in a few days. Don't stray from the path and be very careful, because with such a cargo, it could be dangerous to stop too much in the desert. Go see Marcela so she can help you store the things when you arrive — Halsin said in a low voice, trying not to attract attention as he knew that within the confines of Hardwind, law and order were present, but out in the desert, they would be an easy target for anyone who knew they were carrying a human and a Sharq who weren't even warriors.

—Don't worry, Halsin, we'll go straight there without any detours. Thank you very much for your help — said Clarke.

With everything ready and Clarke and Rex mounted on the kura, Rex shouted—Bye Halsin! See you later! — while waving his paws to say goodbye to Halsin. Then, with a jerk of the ropes on the kura, Clarke gave the order to start their first steps on the march to the outskirts of Hardwind.

The two friends left the dwarven city with excitement and traveled through the desert from very early hours, enjoying all the comforts they could have. Both had used a fragment of crystal that kept them cool, had breakfast and hydrated well, had plenty of water, and since the kura was for them alone, they had full shade under a cloth roof that was equipped on these immense mounts. The only discomfort on this trip, and one that Clarke was already beginning to get used to, was listening to Rex's endless stories and games. This time, for a change, he challenged Clarke with riddles as they moved further and further away from the city.

—Hey Clarke, guess what I'm seeing— Rex said excitedly.

—I'm not in the mood for games, Rex. I'm focused on making sure we don't get lost— Clarke said stubbornly, knowing that wouldn't stop Rex from continuing his game.

—I see... I see something sandy and the color of sand

—A dune... — Clarke replied very clearly.

— Okay, okay, very well, here's a harder one. I see... I see a group of small grains of sand rising in large quantities.

—Another dune...— Clarke replied, knowing that the only thing in the entire landscape was dunes and more dunes.

—Wow, Clarke, that's not fair, you're so smart but here's another one...— Rex said, eyeing something in the distance that was growing larger as it approached from the horizon —You won't guess this one, I see something that... that's running really fast, has a curved sword, and looks furious.

—A dune...— Clarke replied almost automatically, but a shiver ran down his spine when he came to his senses and said — Wait! What did you say?

—Oh no, Clarke! It's not a dune, it's something much worse. It looks like a Vor'shak coming towards us — Rex said alarmed.

—A Vor... what? — Clarke asked as he turned to look at the horizon to see what Rex had seen and was so alarmed about.

Clarke observed a humanoid species, a kind of lizard man running very fast through the desert sands. He had scaly skin, a tail with spikes like an iguana's, but larger, and he seemed like a hybrid between a man and a serpent. He was heading towards them, holding a scimitar in one hand, as well as terrible claws, a forked tongue, and huge snake-like fangs. He had eyes like a reptile's that reminded them of the lizards so common in Florida; although this creature was much larger and more threatening.

Immediately, Clarke went on high alert and shook the kura's reins to make it go faster, but the speed of the pack animal couldn't compare to the impressive speed of the Vor'shak that was getting closer and closer every second.

Clarke grabbed a sword that Halsin had equipped them with in case a dangerous situation like this arose, although he wasn't a warrior and was terrified, he refused to give up without a fight.

The Vor'shak's arrival was imminent, and when it was already close to the kura, it jumped and mounted it, letting out a serpentine sound in a recognizable language — Shhhh, surrender, and your death will be quick. This kura and all its contents are now mine — Immediately after, it swung its scimitar at Clarke who, luckily and by reflex, blocked it with his sword, but from the impact, he lost his balance and fell from the kura face-first onto the sands of the dune.

Meanwhile, Rex lunged to bite the hand holding the Vor'shak's scimitar, but with a strong struggle and the claws of his other hand, he struck Rex and knocked him off the kura as well. Following this, the Vor'shak let out a battle roar similar to that of a reptilian beast like a dinosaur, which caught Clarke's attention as he stood up on the sand and spat it out of his mouth.

The lizard man prepared for another attack, and very confidently jumped from the kura towards

Clarke who reflexively put his sword up to cover himself clumsily as he closed his eyes. Luckily, before the Vor'shak could land a direct blow with his scimitar on Clarke, Rex jumped and rammed into the lizard man from the side, causing him to roll on the sand. Rex didn't wait for the Vor'shak to get up and began to wrestle with him, biting him hard.

The two of them tumbled down the dune, rolling over and over. Rex was fiercely biting the Vor'shak while the latter tried to shake Rex off with strong jerks and blows. Clarke was coming to his senses, hurrying to run after his friend who needed help. So, Clarke slid down the dune as fast as he could, his sword in hand. The Vor'shak was about to break free, but Rex insisted on biting him harder to keep him still. Until at one point, the lizard man, tired of the struggle and seeing that the blows of his fists and claws were not deterring the dog/hyena. He used the spikes of his tail and swept Rex aside with a strong movement, sending him flying a few meters away onto the sand.

At that moment, Clarke, who had already caught up with them and, emboldened by his friend, aimed his sword and launched a powerful blow at the Vor'shak, which took part of the impact on its shoulder before it could deflect the rest of the attack with its scimitar. Immediately, the lizard humanoid returned with devastating attacks against Clarke, who could not cover himself at the same speed and ended up receiving a cut on his arm that made him drop his sword and spill blood on the sand.

The Vor'shak, although wounded, had the advantage. It was a beast whose entire life was dedicated to battle, and although it was young, with the rhythm of the battle in its favor, it savored the loot it would obtain from the two friends. However, with his experience far from that of a veteran, he failed to see the stubbornness and impetuousness of Rex to protect his friend, and with a great tug caused by Rex's bite, he found himself once again in a fierce struggle to free his arm from the Sharq's bite.

Clarke, who was not used to having a possibly fatal wound, had been distracted from the fight by watching how the sand under his feet was dyed the red color of his blood, which came from the deep cut that the scimitar had made in his arm. But thanks to the adrenaline of the moment, it took only a few seconds for him to react and pick up his sword to help his friend, who was also wounded, making his last effort to defeat the formidable enemy.

Rex kept his strong bite and shakes on the Vor'shak, who hit and kicked with its free limbs to try to break free. When it seemed like he was managing to tire Rex and start to get loose, Clarke didn't hesitate to take advantage of the few seconds he had and, running, aimed his sword, delivering a thrust from the Vor'shak's back that pierced it from one side to the other. Rex let go at that moment, panting from exhaustion and the pain of his wounds. Just like Clarke, who, due to the shock of delivering that fatal blow, fell sitting on the sand while watching the creature as it finished writhing for the last time before dying on that dune.

It had been an act of survival and self-defense on the part of both friends, but that image was something they disliked, and especially Clarke who had never been in such a situation. But he knew that if it weren't for their luck and teamwork, it would have been them writhing in the sand. At that moment, Rex ran to Clarke, who was still sitting on the sand trying to emotionally recover from the recent event, and said in a very worried voice – Clarke! Clarke, your arm is bleeding a lot!

Clarke turned to look at his arm and noticed that the cut seemed much worse than he felt, although he was beginning to feel more and more pain, and how the blood was painting his entire forearm, hand, and dripping between his fingers. Clarke was no doctor, but anyone who saw that kind of hemorrhage would know that at the rate he was losing blood, Clarke could bleed out in a few minutes.

—Clarke, what do we do? You're really bad, I don't know how to heal you and the nearest healer is in the village of Zira, almost 2 hours from here.

Clarke knew he wouldn't make it to the village alive like that, or at best, conscious. However, he remembered how, in his days as a CoolForever technician, the fire department had visited one day and given them a first aid class on burns and bleeding. At the time, he thought that morning of training was useless, as he wasn't going to be around to save anyone, only the air machines.

But right now, it was the knowledge that would save his life.

Right there, Clarke took a belt, tied it tightly around his arm, close to his body, before the wound, and secured it in a way that created a tourniquet to stop the bleeding and give him time to make it to the village alive. Rex watched in awe as Clarke performed this maneuver and gradually calmed his panic. However, he was also injured, not seriously, but with bruises and cuts that hurt quite a bit.

Clarke, partially and temporarily stable, stood up and, looking at his friend, asked — Rex, friend, are you okay? Let me help you too — after that, he put some bandages on him and they both quickly climbed onto the kura that was a dune away where it was waiting for them.

—We beat him, Rex! We gave him what he deserved...— Clarke said in a trembling voice as he noticed his injured arm starting to go numb and feel cold.

— Thanks for healing me, Clarke, but don't talk or worry anymore. I'll take care of things from now on, please try not to move too much until we get to the village. I'll make this kura run like the fastest in the desert.

At that moment, Rex shook the kura's reins with force and it started to move forward —Come on, kura! Show me what you're made of! – Rex said, showing his desperation to the pack animal which, in a strange animal-to-animal connection, seemed to understand his desperation and hurried (as much as biology allowed) its steps to move faster.

Clarke, lying on the rug that was in the transport area of the kura, began to feel how the adrenaline was wearing off and his wounds were stealing his attention. Clarke didn't want to die, nor lose his arm, he knew he had about two hours before the damage was irreversible. He prayed for the kura to move forward as he began to faint from the blood loss he had already suffered.

— ¡Clarke stay with me! don't fall asleep – said Rex as he suffered watching his friend in that state and overwhelmed by the uncertainty of whether he would make it to the village in time.

The long journey between villages became extremely long, Rex felt as if the journey had lasted weeks and as if the kura wasn't moving forward no matter how much he demanded it to go fast. Although he knew the animal was giving its best. Everything was a desperation until, finally, he managed to see the village of Zira. As soon as they approached, Rex couldn't wait any longer and got off the kura with Clarke, who he carried unconscious on his back, and ran towards Marcela's house

—Marcela, please, I need your help!— Rex said excitedly as he entered the house.

Marcela saw Clarke with his arm and clothes covered in blood and Rex covered in bandages and excited. She immediately assumed they needed an emergency doctor —Follow me Rex, I know who can help you.

Rex followed her quickly as they both ran to another house at the end of the village. Upon entering that shop, a young elf with many sun tattoos on her hands and face greeted them.

—What happened? Poor creatures — said the elf as she received Clarke and arranged for a human assistant to attend to Rex on the next bed.

—A Vor'shak attacked us when we were coming here from the village of Hardwind, please, Marcela, take care of the kura that brought us, Halsin sent some things — said Rex as he was being attended to and began to faint from the smell of the medicine and because his blood pressure was starting to decrease, now everything was in the hands of the healers.

Both friends were treated by the elf's incredible skills, who thanks to a very rare ability could heal the wounds of living beings with a white crystal. Once she held it in her hands, it radiated a light that illuminated the wounded area and gradually stopped the bleeding, closed the wounds, and repaired the cells of the different layers of the skin. On the elf's face, one could see the physical and spiritual effort it required of her.

Marcela didn't waste any time, and seeing that the two friends were being attended to by the specialists inside the village, she went to attend to the kura that Halsin had sent, since, without knowing exactly, she already assumed that it had materials and objects of value that were better treated with discretion.

As the hours passed, Clarke woke up lying on the bed in the healing house and watched as the elf conversed with Rex who looked recovered and Marcela, who had a face of intrigue.

— A Vor'shak attacked you? And alone? Those beasts are the worst. It's a good thing you survived and managed to get here before Terissa could heal you — said Marcela, showing a face that expressed how she was analyzing this terrible event.

— Clarke, you're awake! That's great – said Rex excitedly.

—Don't move too much, Clarke, and please, Rex be gentle with him, he just woke up from a very complex surgery – said Terissa, happy to see him recovered.

Clarke sat up on the bed and noticed that his arm no longer hurt, he didn't even have a scar. He was very surprised because he thought for sure they would have had to amputate it. He looked at Terissa with great joy and said — I don't know how you did it, but thank you very much.

—You're welcome, Clarke, it's all thanks to the god of crystals who blessed me with this special ability to heal people and creatures in need – replied Terissa, showing her devotion.

—Clarke, now that you're awake, I have questions for you. Do you think you could come with me and Rex to my house? – Marcela asked.

Clarke nodded, and feeling good and pain-free, he stood up to walk with Rex and her out of Terissa's house and towards Marcela's shop. On that journey, Clarke told her everything about the attack and how they had luckily survived. Marcela, upon finishing listening to the story, whistled loudly using two fingers on her lips.

Instantly, a Sharq like Rex entered the shop, looked at him disdainfully and with an air of superiority, and said —Marcela, you called me, what do you need? — the Sharq said.

—Hi Max, can you detect the smell of any Vor'shak on Clarke? — Marcela asked, pointing at Clarke.

—Let me get a good whiff of him and I'll confirm it — Max said very confidently. Then he proceeded to sniff Clarke. At that moment, Clarke felt a little uncomfortable. Why were they sniffing him? Did they not believe his story?

Max stopped sniffing Clarke and with his ears perked up, he pointed in one direction and said —I smell it, it's in that direction — he said referring to his ears that were slightly tilted.

—You know what to do, Max— said Marcela and after that, Max ran out of the house.

Rex, with a bit of indignation, said — Why didn't you ask me? I could have done that too.

—I don't doubt it, Rex, but you've had enough of fighting those beasts for a while, and Max is an expert in those tracking and combat situations — said Marcela confidently.

Clarke didn't understand what had happened, and why Marcela had sent one of her best trackers to follow the trail of the dead Vor'shak, and couldn't help but express his confusion clearly on his face. Before he could say anything, Marcela spoke — Clarke, that Vor'shak attack is strange, they almost never travel alone and I just want to make sure its companions aren't nearby. You were very lucky to survive facing a creature like that. It's a good thing it probably got overconfident seeing you as easy prey and was mistaken. I'm very surprised you survived knowing you're not even a warrior apprentice.

—Yes... Rex saved me, I couldn't have defeated the lizard man without him.

—By the way, Halsin got ahead of you and sent me a message urgently using the black crystals, he told me what they intend to do —Marcela pointed to a small box where the small black crystal was located and continued — In case you're interested, it's through these crystals that we can send short messages immediately and over long distances. You speak into them and once you close the box, the other party opens it and receives the message. Few people have the black crystal communication system, I can say that, for me, it's one of the advantages of being in charge of this village.

Clarke was surprised by the different possible uses of those crystals and at the same time by all of Marcela's story, which made it clear to him that he would have to be cautious with all those strange creatures outside the village. He was already starting to lose count of how many times he had been in danger.

—Halsin told me what you plan to create and I think it will be fabulous for the village, but many others may not see it as good and may want to prevent you from building it at all costs, Clarke. Your life may be in danger. Please keep all your activities secret and count on me for whatever you need, okay?– said Marcela, warning that she would do her best to keep the village in order, but dangers from unknown sources were difficult to prevent.

—Thank you for telling me Marcela, I will undoubtedly have to learn to be more discreet and cautious. Don't worry, this isn't going to stop me. My life has been in danger many times since I arrived in Zal and almost all of these times without even knowing if I wanted to create this machine. If there is any danger, I will avoid it, I will build the machine and they won't be able to stop me — said Clarke determined to succeed in his mission.

—Very brave, Clarke, I like you more and more —Marcela smiled — I'll give you one of our biggest houses so you can carry out your project. The kura that Halsin sent has already been dismantled and taken to that tent. Just let me know how I can help you and I'll try to provide it for you. Needless to say, this work will be done in secret and only a small group of my most trusted people know about it.

Clarke felt happy to receive all this help and treatment. Apparently everyone believed strongly in him and the creation of this magical air conditioning. Clarke felt that he couldn't let them down and that he could succeed in his mission. He said goodbye to Marcela and together with Rex they retired to rest and prepare with new energies to begin the manufacture of such a longed-for invention.

Chapter 11: It's a Team Effort

Clarke and Rex got up very early that morning and with discretion and enthusiasm headed to the house that had been prepared for them to create the magical air conditioning machine. The house was large and spacious, equipped with various tools, workbenches, good lighting, and open spaces for testing the machinery. There was also a box covered with cloth that was full of blue crystals arranged to be used in the machine's tests.

Clarke observed all this and felt motivated, although at the same time a feeling of uncertainty began to invade him like an overflowing torrent. He, despite having worked with air conditioning all his life and knowing more than one type of system and how to repair them, had never designed one. There were aspects he had never worried about before, and now he had to pay attention to them.

—I'm ready to help you with whatever you need, Clarke. Just tell me what to do and let's start building – said Rex excitedly, but showing his naivety by believing it would be a job of lining up blocks and having magical air.

— Calm down, Rex. Let me think first about where we start. If you want, you can help me by bringing breakfast – said Clarke, looking for a space free of Rex's questions so he could think.

Rex, happy to help, followed Clarke's request and left the house to get breakfast for the two of them. Meanwhile, Clarke was turning things over in his head. He found himself facing the first difficulty of his project. He didn't know where to begin. He tried to remember his studies from his career and remembered W.H. Carrier and how, on Earth, specifically on the East Coast of the United States of North America, he had created air conditioning as he knew it. He also remembered the laws of thermodynamics that explained many things, such as the fact that cold is not created but is the absence of heat and that his machine had to displace those temperatures to condition specific spaces.

He also remembered the appearance of the machines and how they were classified, and he recalled the refrigerant. That was it! The type of refrigerant would be fundamental to designing its parts. The operating scheme could be the same: pipes that cool and heat, fans that help create the transfer of temperature in the air.

Clarke already knew how to create a motor, but he wouldn't know the resistance of the pressures or how big or small it would need to be without first knowing the composition of the crystals and how to compress, move, and use them.

So, like a sailor who finds his bearings again, Clarke decided to start by studying the composition of the crystals. Understanding their pressures and the characteristics of their gaseous and liquid states. However, with this step forward, two new steps backward emerged. Clarke had another problem. To be able to study the characteristics of the crystal gas, he would need a complex machine to test the pressure and gaseous and liquid states of the crystal, as well as some complex mathematical formulas. Clarke set out to try and dedicated himself to writing sketches, drawing diagrams, thinking and racking his brain about how to solve this problem, but it seemed he was stuck and very far from any progress.

Clarke hated feeling incapable of solving problems and, as the hours passed, his frustration led him to scribble over his writings, erase his drawings, and pull at his hair as he threw himself on the floor, contemplating how small he felt faced with such a challenge. Even the breakfast that Rex had brought and that had gone cold on the table didn't improve his mood. What was he going to do? He couldn't simply give up and disappoint everyone; he couldn't bear such a humiliation to his ego. For anything in the world, he didn't want to go back to working in the mines. It seemed that the more he thought about it, the more frustrated he became and he felt as if his body was getting heavier and sinking into the carpet where he had lain down.

Rex was worried about Clarke and constantly made optimistic and positive comments to cheer him up, but he couldn't achieve any effect or the opposite of what he wanted, since sometimes it seemed to annoy him more. So he went out for a while to take a walk around the village.

A short while after finding himself alone and lying on the floor, Clarke took a few deep breaths and stood up. He thought that perhaps a walk in the warm embrace of the outdoors would help him think differently than in his confinement. But just as he was about to go out, he unexpectedly found Terissa entering the house, eager to greet him.

— Hello Clarke, did I come at a bad time? – Terissa asked.

— Hello Terissa, not at all, I just wanted to take a short walk to clear my head about the project.

— If you want, I can come with you. I wanted to know how you were doing and if you were suffering from any side effects – said Terissa, a little embarrassed.

— Of course you can come with me. The truth is, I haven't felt bad so far, unless the side effects have to do with the lack of an idea— said Clarke, looking for an excuse for his slow progress.

—No, the side effects have nothing to do with mental states, they would be related to your wound, if it still hurt or if it had reopened.

Clarke lifted the sleeve of the arm where he had been injured and jokingly said to her – No, no pain yet and no guts coming out of my arm, doctor.

Terissa smiled with a little laugh and said – I'm so glad to see you're doing well. It seems you're not even worried about that.

—Honestly, Terissa, I didn't even know there could be side effects, but yes, I've had more important problems on my mind with the development of the machine. However, I know I told you before and I'll tell you again anyway, thank you very much, Terissa. I'm really in your debt for saving my life, my arm, and healing Rex.

Terissa was a little embarrassed by such sincere gratitude, as the people of the village are not usually so grateful in their words, since they take medical care for granted and their expectations are always high.

— Don't worry, Clarke, it's my job and I do it gladly. Now that I see you're well, I also wanted to tell you something,' followed these words, Terissa lowered her voice a bit and continued, 'I'm not only the village healer, I also serve as a counselor and recently I've started to see Rex very differently. It's as if he's been infused with the energy of several crystals and filled with life. Poor Sharq used to come to my house a lot seeking advice, always depressed and dull. He didn't get along with anyone and didn't feel useful, he always walked with his ears and head down. The truth is, I always tried to advise him, but he's just like that, very talkative, sincere and innocent. And the truth is that the people of this village are always busy and working hard to keep the village going and also to cope with the heat. So Rex is quite a character that people don't usually tolerate for long periods. However, you, since Rex saw you and brought you to the village, it's as if your presence has done him good. Lately I've seen him happier, more energetic, with a sparkle in his eyes. Anyway, I'm telling you this, Clarke, because I saw in your face what you feel, and I want you to be clear that you've been making a very positive change in Rex and I'm sure you'll be able to achieve this project to make an even more positive change in the village.

Clarke was surprised by Terissa's warm words and by learning her perspective; it comforted him and made him feel better. 'No, I hadn't seen it that way. Thank you for letting me know.

— Don't worry, Clarke, it's a pleasure to help you. Now, I'll go back to my house in case someone arrives who needs my skills. See you later.

Clarke waved goodbye with a thumbs-up and a smile. He felt more hopeful as he returned to the house where he was working. When he entered, he found Rex who had a plate of hot food for lunch. — I saw you didn't like the breakfast,

Clarke, but I brought you a chef's specialty, a good kura steak in cream and a delicious salad. I asked the chef for his special dish for my great friend.

Clarke was glad to see Rex and, with a pat on the head as if petting a pet, thanked him and sat down to eat with his friend, who talked about all kinds of dishes and foods he wanted to invite Clarke to try one day.

Once they finished taking that much-needed break, Clarke took paper and pencil and began to write down diagrams and formulas. He racked his brain to remember the laws of physics, the algebra, and the mathematics he had studied years ago. In some parts, he even dared to fill in the gaps with small inventions of calculation to at least try to get closer to a first prototype design. He wanted to succeed, even if it was prototype after prototype or failure after failure, as each mistake was a learning experience.

He didn't want to give up and began to invent ways to make his designs work. However, after several more long hours of work. Like a rocket that takes off but quickly begins to fall to the ground, he realized that he was still not advancing, with nothing useful and no progress. Reality showed him that inventing calculations or formulas to fill in the gaps of the design that he didn't understand or remember would never work.

Clarke felt frustrated again, useless again. This was a big blow to his ego. He couldn't believe that something he had worked on for so many years was so difficult to understand and design. Clarke fell back onto the carpet on the floor of the house and silently contemplated the sketches of his project.

At that moment, a bell that was located at the door sounded, as a way of warning whenever someone opened and closed it. Clarke looked up and saw Marcela who saw him, smiled at him and said — Wow! What a curious way to build a machine — referring to the fact that she had found Clarke lying on the floor without any tools or materials in his hands.

— Oh, it's nothing, I've just run into a couple of problems with the design, among them, that I first need a machine to study the pressures of the crystal and the properties of its physical states — said Clarke as he quickly stood up and tried to hide his lack of progress.

Marcela contemplated the images on the wall and the sketches that Clarke had made. — I don't fully understand what you're writing here, but if you need a machine to put the crystal in and study its properties, there's already something like that — said Marcela in a carefree manner, implying that it wasn't something difficult to get.

Clarke froze, feeling like a complete idiot. All this time of work, of high stress, where he pulled his hair and threw himself on the floor thinking about how to create a way to study the crystal and it never occurred to him that it could have already been created, probably to study this and other crystals — Are you telling me, that you already have a machine that can study the gas of the crystal? — Clarke asked.

— More or less. Crystals have always been important and a mystery, so several machines have been created to work with them. There's one that I have in the shop where I work with the yellow crystals that might be useful to you, they're not for the blue crystals, but you can take a look — said Marcela inviting him to see it.

Clarke wasted no time and practically pushed Marcela out of the house, walking at a hurried pace to where Marcela had that machine. They both walked through the village until they reached a large house from which several metal pipes emerged from the walls and disappeared under the sand. Upon entering, Clarke could see all kinds of machinery working with the yellow crystals. Marcela, who was standing in front of him, gestured with her open hands, pointing to the machinery and said — This is the engine room and power plant that supplies the village with light and energy. It's my baby and you have to admit it's a beauty — she said proudly.

Clarke was speechless, he had never seen such machinery before, but he understood that it was like a kind of power plant and gas station that supplied the village.

Once inside the huge house/workshop, they searched for the machine that most closely matched the characteristics that Clarke needed for his invention. There, Marcela showed him a machine in a corner that had accumulated dust and signs of disuse.

— This is the machine, Clarke. With this one, the gaseous pressures of the yellow crystals were studied. You would have to modify it so that you can also see the liquid pressures of the blue crystal and be able to test the change of state of the crystal's magic — said Marcela.

Clarke was excited, and humbly said — Thank you very much, Marcela. I was in a big bind to start creating the machine. This will help me a lot.

—You're welcome, Clarke. You could have asked. I'm here to help you with that project in whatever you need, don't forget that you can tell me about your progress. I don't know if these things will be useful to you, but I leave them at your disposal.

—Thank you. You're right, for a moment I didn't want to bother you, I know you count on me to succeed.

— You don't bother me, Clarke. I'm happy to help you. The only thing that could bother me is if you give up.

Clarke was excited by Marcela's words. He had to learn to collaborate with others and accept their help. He had to stop assuming and communicate with them. Everything seemed easier now that he knew he wasn't alone.

— Thank you again, Marcela, I appreciate your help and I'm sure I'll count on you when I need help.

— Of course, Clarke, you know where to find me.

Marcela said goodbye and left to attend to other village matters. Clarke, for the moment, not needing any more help, decided to study the machine. To do so, he went to his workshop where he had been working, to collect some papers, crystals, and tools. At that moment, when he was gathering those things, the doorbell rang again.

Clarke looked up again and this time he saw two dwarves. They were Helmir and Björn.

— Hello Helmir, Björn, how are you? I'm glad to see you — said Clarke with surprise and joy, as they were the ones who had saved him from drowning in the electric crystal cave.

— Hello Clarke, good to see you. Halsin told us you were up to something — said Björn with a smile.

— Yes, we've come to lend a hand, a project like this can't be left in the hands of just one man — said Helmir as he approached Clarke and helped him carry the things he was collecting.

—Not just one man, but also a great and trustworthy Sharq — Rex said from a corner, having apparently fallen asleep and waking up just as he heard the conversation.

Clarke let out a small laugh and said, "Yes, Rex, I don't think your great contribution has been questioned. Well, guys, I wasn't expecting more help, but it's certainly welcome — said Clarke, letting them help with the things, then on the way to the electrical machinery workshop, where the pressure machine was, he told them about his progress.

—Wow, now I understand what you're trying to do, it's great that we're here. Well, this machine is a dwarven design and invention, and we'd be happy to help you modify it—Helmir said with great confidence.

Clarke was surprised by Helmir and Björn's abilities and knowledge, and felt humble about himself. At the beginning of the day, he felt like a super mastermind who was bringing a unique invention to this world in every way, but little by little he had realized and reflected that there were already certain steps and inventions made by the inhabitants of this world that could help build the machine if they were organized. Perhaps they hadn't invented air conditioning because of the crystals themselves, which appeased the need to deal with the heat. It was something that Clarke found curious and that at the same time made it clear to him that he wouldn't be the super inventor who would do everything by himself. No, he would need a team to collaborate with, as well as the support of all these people who brought with them knowledge of this world that he didn't have and at the same time the knowledge of his world that only he had.

With a clear mind and new ideas, Clarke took his tools and proceeded to work hard with the brothers to modify the machine to study the blue crystals. Now everything was going well and Clarke felt much better.

Chapter 12: Each to their own Trade

A couple of months passed, and Clarke's team had made significant progress. The machine to study the blue crystal was now a reality, and Clarke was already familiar with its properties such as temperature, characteristics, and behavior.

The team, composed of Clarke, Helmir, Björn, Rex, and occasionally with the support of Marcela, was quite optimistic about their progress and their chances of successfully completing the project.

Clarke was taking notes on the design of his air conditioning machine when he heard the shop bell ring where he worked. A white-bearded dwarf with a distinctive mustache entered. It was Halsin.

—Hello Halsin, it's great to see you — Clarke said as he reached out to shake his hand.

—Hello Clarke, hello everyone — Halsin replied, shaking everyone's hand, even Rex's, who responded with his paw — It's good to see that you've made progress. I see designs and drawings of what looks like the machine, very curious — Halsin said as he looked at the drawings and writing, trying to decipher for himself what the final machine would be like.

Clarke offered to explain what they had been working on, the progress they had made, and the new ideas that would allow them to create the machine.

—I understand— Halsin said, making sure he understood all the information Clarke had given him. — You're saying that these temperatures are so high that if it were an ordinary machine from your world, it wouldn't be able to work for long before being damaged.

—Yes, you're exactly right, Halsin. Luckily, after studying the blue crystals, I realized that they're perfect for cooling spaces even in this hot desert — Clarke replied, very positively.

—That sounds fantastic. Perhaps the gods themselves wanted us to create this machine, Clarke. Watch out, you might be one of their messengers! — he said cheerfully, giving Clarke a hearty slap on the back.

Clarke felt Halsin's heavy hand almost knock the wind out of him, but he didn't get angry. He knew it was a rough manner that all dwarves had and he'd learned that from Helmir and Björn over the past couple of months of living and working together. Then he told Halsin — Right now, we're working on the design of the system to make it work efficiently with the village lifestyle and its layout. We think the most convenient thing will be a large condensing machine that will be located outside the village because it will give off immense heat, and some very thick pipes that will carry the contents of the blue crystals in and out of the shops to extract the heat from them and cool them down.

Halsin was amazed. It seemed like everything could work perfectly. But considering the high pressures, the size of the machine, and the working temperatures it would reach, he scratched his beard and said — A machine like that could only work with a metal that can withstand such temperatures and be resistant. We would need a good amount of solar metal — After saying that, Halsin fell into a long silence.

Clarke had noticed until then that there were different metals and some chemical compounds different from his world, but many were similar to those he already knew and understood that an ordinary metal wouldn't withstand such temperatures without melting or losing its resistance.

— I think I know how to get a large shipment, but it will take me some time to organize my contacts. I'll send you a shipment to get you started and another later — Halsin finished saying, then he said goodbye to Clarke and called Helmir aside to talk outside the shop. After a while Helmir came back alone and informed Clarke — I'll leave you with Björn, I'm going to bring the first shipment of metals so we can start building that wonderful cooling machine you call a machine - After that, Helmir hugged his brother and said goodbye.

Once again, the team got to work and perfected their designs and calculations to be able to build the first prototype of the magical air conditioning machine. Luckily, they didn't have to stop their progress for when a shipment of metals arrived in the village.

The inhabitants of Zira were already questioning so much activity and cargo of things to the same house/workshop where Clarke and his team were working on their secret project.

Marcela, as the village leader, was responsible for dispelling rumors and inventing others to keep people's noses out of where they didn't belong, as she knew that this machine would be revolutionary and would decrease their great dependence on blue crystals. Something that for some people, instead of a blessing, would mean a great tragedy.

Clarke and his team continued with the work and began to materialize it using the shipment of solar metal that Halsin had sent, although to their surprise, this shipment did not arrive in the hands of Helmir, but of three other dwarves named Balh, Manny, and Harold who showed up willing to help.

Clarke welcomed them and, organizing the team and showing his appreciation for what each one contributed to the creation of the machine, they continued with their progress and work.

There came a point where they had to start welding different pieces that they had designed for the machine. Clarke was a good welder, as in his years of work as a technician, he had welded innumerable times from the smallest to the largest air conditioning machines. However, he began to have many difficulties with the welding of this solar metal. The torch he needed to weld it reached temperatures so hot that Clarke had never known before and it was quite complicated. So much so, that at one point he delegated the work to Björn, then to Balh, Manny, and Harold, but, although all the dwarves are usually skilled in metalwork, there was something about this metal that turned out to be difficult to weld. It was difficult to heat, but at the same time, once hot, it was very easy to melt and damage.

Clarke felt frustrated that he couldn't do it and that his team wasn't showing a different result. What had started as a new challenge that seemed like a piece of cake was turning into a big annoyance. Hours passed and then night until the next day the team was stuck on the same problem.

Clarke decided to stop for a moment and take a walk around the village. Sometimes walking and looking at those two suns, which seemed like the two eyes of some giant or divine being watching him, filled him with courage, but also helped him clear his mind.

On the walk, Rex joined him, and he saw how Clarke's face showed the expression of someone facing a dilemma.

—Hey Clarke, this isn't the first obstacle we've faced and that we've eventually found a solution for, and it won't be the last either — Rex said, trying to cheer him up.

—Yeah, Rex, but this one seems different. We can't waste the material that Halsin got us, who knows how much it cost him to get it. Besides, it's been almost 8 months since I arrived in this world. I can't afford to waste any more time.

—Well, that metal must be very expensive, I've only heard of the existence of that metal once and it's because it's the same one used in the core of the central machine that the village uses to process the electrical magic of the yellow crystals —Rex said without realizing the relevant information he knew and had just said. Then he asked — And why do you pay so much attention to the time you've been here since you arrived?

At that moment, Clarke's mind went blank, ignoring Rex's question and analyzing the information that Rex had dropped like a bomb in the innocent comment. Clarke felt as if a light bulb had gone off, he felt he had found a possible solution and then asked — What did you say, Rex?

— That it wasn't the first or last challenge we'd have to overcome.

— No, no, after that

— That that metal is very expensive — said Rex, wagging his tail.

— No! You said that this metal had already been used in the central machine that supplies the village with electricity. That is, someone has already welded it and worked it as they wanted. Do you know who it was?

—Ahhhh.... - said Rex, realizing he had said something important — Yes, yes I know who it was. It was Marcela's father.

With those words, Clarke and Rex set off on a fast-paced walk towards Marcela's house. Clarke couldn't contain his excitement. Once there, upon passing through the front door, they found Marcela curiously welding some pipes that constantly needed reinforcement and that transported the electricity from the yellow crystals.

—Hi, Marcela, I need your help — said Clarke excitedly.

—Hi Clarke, how's the project going? – Marcela asked as she finished her welding.

— We've had problems welding the solar metal, it melts very quickly and we can't prevent it from being damaged. Rex told me that maybe you know how to weld it.

Marcela turned off her torches, removed her protective glasses, and wiped the dirt off her face. — Let me tell you, Clarke, that you found the right person — she said with a confident smile.

Clarke, with great joy and anticipation, helped her gather her things and they went together to the shop where he was working on the construction of the machine. There, the other members of the team were discussing and still couldn't weld the metal correctly.

Marcela passed by and waved them aside, saying — Let a master show you how it's done. — Then she proceeded to put on her safety glasses and turn on her torches.

Clarke watched her with admiration and at the same time feeling a bit jealous. Inside, he wished he could have taken the spotlight of the welding, but he couldn't deny that, in view of his attempts and failures, it was a relief to have gotten help.

Seeing Marcela's attitude reminded him of himself sometimes when he was arrogant with the technicians he trained at CoolForever. Dominating every situation regarding air conditioning machines in Florida. However, he understood that it was one thing to act that way with confidence and respect as Marcela did, and another thing was how repeatedly Clarke behaved rudely and arrogantly towards his former apprentices, new employees, and other experienced technicians. He was ashamed of that memory and tried to focus his gaze on what Marcela was doing.

Marcela began confidently working with the peculiar metal. She had a lot of experience welding all kinds of metals in this world, although this was not the most common. She began by regulating the flame of her torches so that it was as dispersed or focused as she wanted, continuing to heat the metal slowly, playing it safe. However, even someone as experienced as her showed a bit of damage when welding. Nevertheless, maintaining her composure and with great determination, she managed to do a decent job.

The weld wasn't perfect, but it worked for the job. Once the welding was finished, Marcela turned off her torches and removed her goggles, saying — Wow, I must have been a long time without seeing a solar metal, but I don't remember my father mentioning that it was so inconsistent when it started to melt, I mean, it seemed to heat up in different parts at different temperatures, now I understand why everyone suffered when they tried to weld it.

Everyone was surprised by Marcela's performance and at the same time felt a little better about themselves knowing that even she had a bit of difficulty performing the weld.

Clarke thanked Marcela and, admiring all the already welded pieces, it was time to assemble them, screw them together, and shape the machine. For that, his team was more than prepared. Among them, Björn said — Well, finally it's time to hit the hammer, I was going crazy if we kept getting stuck on the welding watching the fire like flies — Everyone smiled at hearing his comment. They felt the same way, having spent so much time stuck on that part of the process and now they were back in control of moving forward with their project.

The team started working and getting down to business, between hammering and moving pieces from one side to the other, Björn asked Harold to please refill the beer jugs. To which Harold took a large empty container and left the shop to refill it.

Clarke wasn't a big fan of the idea of consuming alcohol during any kind of work. Initially, he felt it was like an insult to the seriousness of his labor. But he realized that it helped boost the morale of his group, and besides, this work or the norms of this world couldn't be compared to those of Earth. Clarke had learned to understand his team and to respect this, which, although it was against his principles, he had understood was something cultural among the dwarves and he couldn't deny them.

Hours passed and the team continued working until late at night. However, they stopped when they realized that Harold hadn't returned with the beer and the team refused to work dry.

Clarke and the others found it strange, to which Balh said — I'm sure Harold kept the whole jug for himself, knowing that we're almost finished for today.

The team didn't give it much importance as it seemed like something that could be typical of Harold. They gathered their things and Clarke looked one last time at his almost finished air conditioning machine before closing the workshop. With great pride and joy, he observed it, thinking that tomorrow could be the day to turn it on and make it work.

Chapter 13: Threads in the Shadows

Clarke and Rex left the hut where they were sleeping very early in the morning. The excitement of being so close to finishing the machine helped them jump out of bed and go out with a lot of energy. They walked excitedly to where their machine was located. Today, if everything went according to plan, they would finish the magical air conditioning machine.

When they arrived at the workshop, they found Björn and Balh, who informed them that Manny had gone out to look for Harold since they hadn't seen him all night.

Clarke was worried, as they were part of the team, but at the point where they were, it wouldn't be much of a delay. They could still continue with the work.

The team took their tools and focused on the machine again. Clarke connected the electrical tubes, Björn and Balh made sure to assemble the motors, blades, and heavy parts, and Rex passed them the water and beer jugs that Balh and Björn had brought.

Half a day passed like this. As Clarke was giving the machine the final hammer blows and connecting the last piece, he climbed down a 20-foot ladder and looked at the machine they had built with admiration. It was gigantic, imposing, and a marvel of engineering. It was a reflection of the best his team had achieved, and he was very proud to have finally finished it. Now they just had to turn it on and make sure everything stayed together.

Björn saw the joy on Clarke's face and, sharing the same feeling, approached him with Balh and Rex to toast their achievement.

Clarke, who didn't drink during work, couldn't help but feel excited about their accomplishment and decided it was a good idea to join in the toast. Together they clinked their jugs and took a drink of the beer. Clarke hadn't tasted it before, and immediately felt how the temperature of the hot beer (as hot as coffee) didn't allow him to drink it quickly and gave him time to focus on its bitter taste, much more bitter than any beer he had ever tasted before. He definitely thought these dwarves were crazy barbarians for being able to drink so much hot beer in a desert as hot as Zal. After that sip, he discreetly dumped the rest of his jug in time to see Björn and Balh finish theirs as if they had been drinking water.

Björn, still wiping the foam from his mustache, said — Well, now I'm going to look for the lost ones, Manny and Harold. I can't believe they're missing the moment when we turn on this machine. Will you help us Clarke? The sooner we find them, the better.

Clarke looked at his machine one more time as if saying with his eyes, with a touch of affection —I'll be right back, just wait a little longer — And he agreed to help in the search for Harold and Manny. To do so, he turned to Rex and said— Rex, my friend. Do you think you can smell either of them?

—Of course, Clark— He replied—I can smell their beer-soaked sweat from here to the sun. Follow me.

Clarke, Björn, and Balh followed Rex out of the tent and through the village. As they advanced, it made no sense that both dwarves would be heading in a direction that had nothing to do with the beer they were originally looking for.

They continued to follow the trail Rex was sniffing and it led them out of the village — That's strange, why would they leave the village?— Clarke said.

—Maybe your sense of smell is damaged, Rex?— Björn asked.

Rex replied immediately and very confidently — Believe it or not, you are in the presence of the best nose in all of Zal.

Björn let out a small laugh but decided to leave the animal alone and follow him as his most reliable clue for rescuing his friends.

—Be very careful, we don't know what we're going to find — said Balh.

The group followed the trail with Rex. They all crossed the desert dunes under the immense heat of Zal, but thanks to the help of the blue fragments they had in abundance for the construction of the machine, they were a little relieved.

As they advanced and moved away from the village, the suspicion that something was wrong was more than evident. The duo of dwarves pulled out their hammers, prepared to face whatever came their way, and handed one to Clarke so that he wouldn't be defenseless.

At that moment, Clarke was surprised. They weren't giving him that hammer to build anything; it was for fighting, to defend himself against whatever threat had been the reason for his companions' disappearance —What the hell are we getting ourselves into? — Clarke wondered as he imagined all kinds of dangers like the Fire Gnomes or the Vor'shak.

— We've reached a point where the trail stops — Rex raised his head and said — I can smell them, we're close — He pointed to a small rocky cave ahead.

The team became alert and cautiously entered. They quickly realized that the place wasn't very deep and that on its rocky floor were Manny and Harold, bound hand and foot and with their faces covered with a dark cloth bag.

—Damn it! What happened to you, Manny, Harold? Answer! — Björn shouted as he ran with Balh to untie them.

Without wasting any time, they removed the bags from their faces and observed the alive, although beaten, faces of both.

—Are you alright, friend? — Balh asked Harold.

—Yeah... but... I need beer — Harold replied weakly, his lips covered in sand.

Clarke observed this with relief to see that they were okay but was worried —Who did this to you? — He asked.

—They've been watching us this whole time. They followed me when I went looking for Harold and ambushed me. They were other Dwarves — said Manny as he recovered.

—Those bastards, they must have been from Asher's group. They've always hated Halsin for his ideas. Did they tell you what they wanted?— Björn said.

—No, they just caught me and threw me in here, where I found Harold— said Manny.

Clarke analyzed the situation and said — That's strange. Why would someone want to just ambush them, tie them up, and leave them in this cave?

Clarke's doubts were well-founded. If someone wanted to harm them, they could have simply killed them once they were tied up or buried them in the desert sands. Or, if they wanted a ransom, they could have contacted Clarke and his team and hidden the captured companions better. The fact that they were found so quickly and in a relatively safe place, far from the heat of the sun and predators, was quite strange.

Björn, in that moment of deduction, said—I think I understand what's going on. Someone found out what we're designing. Clarke, you have to go to the village now, I'll take care of these two. You go with Rex and Balh to make sure the workshop is okay.

Clarke heard those words and a shiver ran down his spine. He had to go to the village immediately. He started running with Rex and Balh to get there as soon as possible. Maybe this had all been a trap and they had all fallen for it.

When they reached the outskirts of the village, a large black plume of smoke rose into the sky, the villagers were running with water containers from side to side. Clarke's heart raced —Where is that fire coming from? What happened? — he wondered. As they got closer, he felt more and more fear and anxiety until he was confronted with a heartbreaking sight.

—No... It can't be — Clarke said in a tone of voice that reflected as if his soul had left his body and returned, leaving a great feeling of hopelessness and despair.

Clarke stood before the workshop where he had poured so much time and effort over the past few weeks and months. The workshop, which housed the air machine and all his designs, papers, and schematics, was completely engulfed in flames. People were trying to put out the fire, but it was useless. Among them was Marcela, who was running back and forth with containers of water, trying to extinguish the blaze.

Without a second thought, Clarke started moving towards the burning building, attempting to enter. Seeing this, Rex ran after Clarke and shouted —Clarke, don't do this! Are you crazy? You can't go in there, you'll get burned!

Clarke continued forward, ignoring Rex and simply said— Everything is in there, Rex! If it burns, we'll be worse off than when we started!— With that, Clarke soaked himself with water and tried to enter the fire to salvage what he could of his work. But Rex, biting at his clothes, managed to stop him.

Clarke tried to struggle against him, but at that very moment, a concentration of air and fire inside the workshop caused an explosion that sent him flying backward, landing in the sand next to Rex.

—Clarke, see why I told you? Your life is worth more than those papers and schematics. We can try again later — said Rex.

Clarke was out of his mind at that moment. He was overwhelmed by a storm of emotions: frustration, anger, denial, among others. He couldn't think clearly, and a torrent of catastrophic thoughts flooded his mind: "Everything is lost", "Now you won't be able to go back to your world", "All that work and sacrifice for nothing", "You're a failure." Clarke was lost in that sea of thoughts and the bright glow of the fire that consumed everything Clarke and his team had achieved.

—Here he is! We've got one of the bastards who started the fire — Clarke heard from a distance.

The shout brought him back to his senses, focusing the rage that burned within him. He was eager to unleash it on whoever had caused such devastation. Clarke grabbed a hammer that was within reach and stormed towards the source of the voice.

Rex ran up to Clarke and snatched the hammer from his hand with a bite —Clarke, what do you think you're doing? That's not like you.

—Rex, give me that hammer back. Don't start interfering and being a nuisance like you always do. Be a good dog and give me that hammer.

—No, Clarke, you're not yourself. You're not thinking clearly.

—And who are you? My fucking psychiatrist? — Clarke said furiously. Immediately, he began to struggle with Rex to take the hammer from him.

They both pulled with all their might, neither giving in. Clarke could only hear and imagine how the person who had started the fire was laughing and might escape without facing the consequences. This filled him with even more rage.

—Stop getting in the way, Rex! Stop being a nuisance!— With that, Clarke forcefully snatched the hammer away and kicked Rex out of his way.

Rex looked at him, sad and disappointed by the attitude and violence with which Clarke had fought for the hammer and what he was about to do. Clarke's words hurt him deeply, and he decided to listen to him and "not be a nuisance." Keeping a little distance, but still following him. Because he still cared about him.

Clarke walked among the people, who were still all alarmed by the fire. He strode with heavy steps and a lot of energy. He carried a rage and a desire to vent his frustration on the "poor" soul who had caused the fire. At a quick pace, he followed the direction from which the call had come.

When he got closer, he saw that it was a hooded humanoid figure heading towards the outskirts of the village, shouting— Quick, he's getting away!

With his adrenaline and cortisol at their peak, Clarke didn't hesitate for a moment to chase after the figure, who was moving faster and faster and starting to run.

The chase, now directed outside the village, led Clarke to follow two humanoid figures who were disappearing behind the nearest dune. One of them was the hooded figure who continued to encourage Clarke to pursue the alleged arsonist who had caused the destruction of the workshop and all its contents.

After climbing and descending a couple of these dunes on the outskirts, Clarke managed to catch up to the hooded figure who had a second humanoid figure pinned to the ground. Clarke gripped the hammer tightly in his hand and approached to observe the face of the arsonist. However, as he stood beside the hooded figure, he was in for a terrible surprise. The face of the man on the ground looked up at him, smiling, and the subject who had encouraged him to follow, also smiled at him with a malicious look.

Both men turned to Clarke, with cables and chains, intending to attack him. Surprised, Clarke tried to defend himself with the hammer and swung a blow at one of the subjects, but missed.

At that moment, one of the two attackers whistled, and from a nearby dune, more hostile figures began to approach. Clarke found himself in a tight spot and tried to get away, but they were starting to surround him, and it seemed like violence was the only option.

Luckily, from one side of the dune, at high speed, Rex arrived to support him, running with determination and power. He reached Clarke and with a bite attacked one of the closest malicious subjects.

Clarke did not waste this timely intervention of Rex and while the companion of the bitten subject was surprised, Clarke managed to land a solid blow with the hammer, knocking him unconscious on the sand. Afterwards, he went on guard and prepared for the multiple subjects who were approaching. Rex, who had also neutralized the other enemy, positioned himself beside Clarke to support him.

Many figures of different sizes and races surrounded them. It seemed that among the attackers were dwarves, elves, and humans. The situation was critical for the two companions who were outnumbered, and it worsened when two corpulent figures stood in front of them and revealed their orcish features.

As they closed in, Rex leaped to bite one, but with a solid blow, they reduced Rex to something like a fly. Clarke didn't hesitate and with his hammer struck one of the orcs. They were so tall that the blow only managed to hit its chest, though he had aimed for the head. The orc reacted as if nothing had happened and with a powerful blow landed a hook on Clarke's jaw, sending him flying backward and falling to the ground, almost immobilized.

Amidst the sound of laughter, the sight of Rex knocked out on the ground, and surrounded by attackers, Clarke felt a great despair, but his body, numb from the blow, wouldn't respond.

At that moment, his vision blurred as they covered his head with a black sack. With a strong, quick, and solid pressure that he felt on the back of his neck, he fell unconscious and at the mercy of his captors.

Chapter 14: Unexpected Allies

The engulfing fire consumed the mechanical workshop as an immobilized Clarke watched, as it devoured the last hope of recovering what was once the project of his life. Clarke saw himself reflected in the flames as they grew larger and more radiant.

Suddenly, his gaze focused on his arms, on his skin, covered in sand, slowly beginning to succumb to the effects of the fire, causing first, second, and third-degree burns.

Terror seized Clarke, who, still motionless, watched as the fire ravaged his skin, making him feel the heavy, burning air in his lungs, which filled him with despair and a sense of being lost.

Once again, Clarke's gaze focused on the fire in front of him. This time, it was no longer consuming the workshop in Zira. Instead, the flames were consuming the engine room on the rooftop of the building where he worked the day of the accident, before arriving in Zal.

Clarke, still burning, watched in pain and despair as, inside that room, his son Alejandro was burning and screaming for his father — Dad, help me! Why did you leave me alone? You're never there when I need you most!

In the fire, he also saw Mr. Jones shouting at him — Clarke, I trusted you! Why, with so much potential, did you let this happen?

He also saw his former coworkers and friends — This is all your fault, Clarke, look where you've brought us all!

Clarke was overwhelmed by guilt, pain, and the memory of all the misfortune that had been brought about by many of his actions. He struggled to watch as the image of those people was consumed by the flames. He blurred his vision for a moment as he began to succumb to the excruciating pain of his burns, and raised his gaze once more, this time looking at Rex, who was also surrounded by flames, and saying to him — I believed in you, Clarke, but in the end, the most important thing has been your work, your project, and not those who were with you, in the end? Is that what I am to you? A nuisance?

Behind Rex, amid the flames, he could see the charred bodies of Marcela, Björn, Halsin, Balh, Harold, and more people from Zal.

Clarke felt lost and disappointed in himself, paralyzed by the horrific scene and almost consumed by the darkness that the flames generated as they covered everything around him in black smoke. As he was about to close his eyes and let himself be consumed by the fire, he heard a voice.

— This is a vision of where the path you've been following will lead you. It's the road you continue on, abandoned, Clarke, but you still have time to change and save yourself and others from this tragic end. It's in your hands— said a mysterious voice, but he knew it came from behind him.

Clarke turned quickly to see the source of these words, but through the thick smoke and the intense heat of the fire, his vision blurred before he could fully discern the humanoid figure in polished shoes, pressed pants, and an immaculate white coat.

At that moment, Clarke woke up, drenched in sweat, and with difficulty observed the face of an elf who was removing the black sack from his head.

— It's time to get up, sleepyhead. Honestly, I wasn't going to keep listening to those screams you were making while you were asleep. The Vor'shak were already thinking of cutting your throat just to shut you up — said the elf, who stood up and pointed Clarke in the direction where those Vor'shak were.

Clarke got up from the arid floor and noticed that he was locked in a cage with the elf who had helped him and a group of five Vor'shak who were glaring at him.

The cage where he was confined seemed to be located in a valley in the desert, between walls of rocky tunnels that rose up and fortunately provided shade over their location.

Clarke, covered in sweat, stood there, still confused about how he had gotten there, and noticed many other cages around him, many with other Vor'shak, and in one of them, his friend Rex who was still unconscious.

Seeing this, Clarke began to bang on the cage door violently, but he couldn't open it or move it, only hurting his hands against the strong steel.

— I doubt a weak human like you can open an orc steel cage, not even I, a superior race, could do it, so do us all a favor and stay calm, human— said the elf from a corner of the cage.

Wrapped in despair and anger, Clarke ignored the elf's words and continued trying to open the cage while shouting — Damn it! This can't be the end, my family needs me, my friends need me, the village needs me, and I can't allow myself to stay here, in this damn cage while everything goes to hell.

Clarke's kicking and struggling against the door continued stubbornly. Faced with this, the elf, surprised by this act of recklessness and despair, jumped to stop Clarke, grabbing him from behind and immobilizing him with a hold on his arms and shoulders.

— Have you lost your mind, human? You won't be able to open the door that way, you'll only get us killed faster. The only reason they haven't done it yet is probably because they're waiting for more prisoners or some slave trader to buy us.

Clarke was surprised and reluctantly relaxed his muscles so the elf would let go of him. Then he looked at him and said —I can't stay here, there's too much at stake. I need to get out of here and make the person responsible for this and the fire at my workplace pay for what they did, then I'll go back to my project — A look of desperation and anger at the person responsible for his misfortune could be seen on his face.

Noticing Clarke's desperation and his interest in resuming this "project," the elf was curious – What project are you talking about, human? Maybe I could help you if the price is right.

—I guess some help would be good if someone could get us out of here to start.

—Well, human, you're lucky today, the great Elliott is in the same cage as you, and I don't plan to rot in here. But that luck depends on the right price — said the elf shrewdly.

Clarke knew that the blue crystals were the currency of Zal and that he had a few of them at the time of his capture. If they managed to escape and find them, he could offer them to Elliott — You know, if you really do manage to get us out of here and to safety, the blue crystals I had with me and that the guards have can be yours.

—What's stopping me from just escaping, getting those crystals for myself, and going off on my own?

Clarke had no clear answer to that, but he tried to tug at the elf's inner strings — Nothing's stopping you, but this world, at least this region of Zal, needs me and counts on me to finish a project that will help many people. I need to get out of here for the sake of many people.

Elliott was surprised by this, it didn't make him feel compassion, but it did pique his curiosity, and Elliott was a very curious elf — What kind of important project could a human be involved in? I need to know if it's worth the trouble of helping you when we escape

— It's a secret, but I guess under these circumstances I have no choice. I'm building a machine that will help many people and change part of life in this desert. With it, there won't be as much dependence on the blue crystals, and people will be able to be in enclosed spaces with more pleasant temperatures. Thus saving many lives and making them easier to bear in this hostile desert.

Elliott didn't know what to think. Such a machine seemed like an impossible invention, too unreal and too good to be true. All his life he had suffered from the relentless and hostile heat of Zal, always needing the coveted crystals to survive its direct exposure. He didn't believe much of Clarke's story, but at the same time seeing the face of this man who had said all this showing determination, confidence and security; created a small doubt in the elf. In a world where magic exists, could a mechanical invention like air conditioning be so unthinkable?

Elliott decided to trust the human who was so determined to escape and achieve justice and finish his project, and agreed to help him. 'Such an invention is undoubtedly needed, if what you say is true, I think I can perhaps help you, human. It's not cheap but I'm sure we can reach an agreement. I know a skilled individual who can get us out of here and a good group of mercenaries and warriors who could stop all these captors and give them what they deserve, and even more so if there's a payment involved.

—What do you have in mind?— Clarke asked, ready to proceed with whatever plan the elf had for their escape.

—Easy. You've got the most skilled elf in the business of escape that Zal has ever seen, and I have the support of these five Vor'shak who would be willing, for some great blue crystals, to get out of here and beat the crap out of those henchmen of Asher who captured us.

—Wait, you know Asher?

—Who doesn't? That scum is always playing dirty and taking out anyone who gets in the way of his crystal business. I'm sure an invention like yours would drive him crazy. In fact, I'm pretty sure that's why you're locked up here. But don't worry, I plan to pay him a visit with all these Vor'shak when we're free.

Clarke was surprised. He hadn't expected to find people so eager to stop Asher's misdeeds. It was certainly a relief to know this, because he could never finish his air project if Asher tried to sabotage it again.

— Well, we'll get out of this cage and free the other Vor'shak. With such a large group, we'll lock up all these captors and go to Asher's base to give him what he deserves, steal his crystals and everyone will be happy. The truth is, they captured me trying to get information and crystals in one of his settlements before, but it has given me the opportunity to meet a few people who are also interested in doing the same thing. And now that you're here. If you offer us all the crystals in your bag, perhaps we can have tangible proof that we will get more of the loot stolen from Asher and his people.

Clarke analyzed the situation and said— You've got a deal, we'll get out of here safely, then we'll go where Asher is and you, together with the Vor'shak, will give him a little street justice.

— That's how it will be, human. Don't worry, this plan is foolproof and a cell like this is no obstacle for the great Elliott, the cunning desert traveler and treasure hunter. You wait for my signal and we'll get out of here together.

— Alright Elliott, I'll wait for your signal. By the way, my name is Clarke. Thanks for offering to help.

— It's a pleasure doing business with you, Clarke— said Elliott, who went with the Vor'shak to tell them about his escape plan and the loot of blue crystals that Clarke had offered them.

After that conversation, everyone in the cage remained very quiet and calm so that the opportunity to escape would present itself. Clarke was attentive, but completely clueless as to how the escape would be. Would they attack a guard and take his key? Would Elliott be waiting for reinforcements? Or maybe he had some magical power? All the questions were swirling around Clarke's head, although one thing was clear. At the moment of action and running, he would have to be ready for anything. Getting out alive and together with Rex was his priority. Clarke was sitting looking at his friend from the other cage, still unconscious but alive. He felt guilty and sorry for him and for why because of him he had dragged him into this situation, but, at least now he could see him feeling a small spark of hope, because, he was going to do whatever it took to fix the situation and take responsibility for the consequences that his actions had caused.

Hours passed and everyone in the cage remained calm, except for Clarke, who hadn't wanted to sleep, hoping that the opportunity to escape would present itself and be 100% attentive. However, during these hours of waiting, he thought many times about Rex and the others. He hoped they were okay and that Asher didn't have a surprise for them too. He knew he had to get out of there, resolve the matter with Asher and contact them when he managed to return to Zira.

Other hours passed and it was almost dusk. At that moment a guard walking with a Sharq approached the cage with the leftovers of what seemed to be parts of a Vor'shak's body and threw them in, falling with direct contact with the sand inside the cage.

Clarke was disgusted to see that they were giving the remains of a former prisoner and thought that the same thing could happen to him or Rex. Elliott, on the other hand, approached the pieces thrown on the floor and began to devour one before giving the rest to the other Vor'shak who also seemed not to waste that dose of protein.

While eating, what seemed to be some fingers, Elliott noticed that Clarke was looking at him with disgust and said, still with food in his mouth — Hey, you really must have a lot of crystals and a privileged life if you've never had to satisfy your hunger with whatever you can find.

— Well, I think I'm allergic to that- Clarke replied evasively to avoid giving more explanations.

Elliott finished cleaning the finger he was eating, and left a sharp nail on it — Hey Clarke, I'm ready to escape. Follow me — he murmured while sucking his fingers and signaling to the Vor'shak that they were going to escape.

Clarke became alert and noticed how Elliott skillfully used the claw of the finger he had eaten to open the door lock, once the "click" sounded followed by the lock falling to the floor. The elf opened the door carefully and motioned to Clarke to walk close and crouched.

The suns were setting and the light was beginning to give way, with its double sunset, to the moonless darkness of Zal. Elliott, standing close to Clarke, said — Now listen carefully. This part is crucial. Now we are all together and the guards haven't even noticed. But when I take the bag of crystals everything will go to chaos. Watch carefully where I move, I'll pass you the keys I get so you can help me open the cages, if we don't manage to open them before the guards overtake us and the five Vor'shak can't protect us anymore, you can consider yourself dead — followed by this, Elliott separated from Clarke without even confirming the face of doubt and nervousness that he had.

Elliott went silently and from corner to corner moving until he reached the bag of crystals that several of the guards were guarding. Before approaching completely, the elf saw in a corner a distracted guard, apparently falling asleep. He took advantage of that opportunity and from behind took a dagger that the guard had in his sheath and when he realized it, it was too late. Elliott had stabbed him with the dagger from the jaw to the brain avoiding making any noise.

Clarke watched the attack from afar with disgust, while Elliott turned to him giving him a thumbs-up gesture that everything was alright. The elf continued stealthily from one corner observing the guards who were moving and dancing around the bag, as soon as he saw the opening he threw the bloody dagger at the head of one of those guards and ran as fast as he could and sliding on the sand to take the bag and near it, some keys to some cells.

Clarke was surprised at how fast the elf moved. It was so fast that the guards reacted when Elliott was already running with the bag in hand a few steps away. At that moment the alarms were activated and everyone in the camp picked up their weapons, ready to capture them again alive or dead. (With more chance that it would be dead so that they would not escape).

Clarke turned to see where the Vor'shak were going, they had all taken up weapons and were preparing to protect Clarke and fight the guards. Elliott at that moment threw the keys he had to Clarke from a distance and continued running through the camp in search of more keys.

Clarke with the keys in his hand, raised his gaze and saw how the guards with great ferocity were heading towards him with the raw intention that was projected in each of them, of wanting to cut him into pieces smaller than the grains of sand.

Nerves invaded Clarke, who for a moment stood still, giving the opportunity for one of the guards to raise his scimitar and brandish it towards his neck.

Luckily, one of the Vor'shak managed to block the attack with an axe and turned quickly to

Clarke, saying — Human, wake up! They will kill us all if you don't manage to open those cages quickly!

Clarke reacted and immediately ran through the chaos of the guards trying to catch him and hit him and the Vor'shak who were fighting to protect him. When he finally reached the first nearest cage, he quickly tried to open it with the set of keys he had in his hands. His pulse was not entirely steady and the nerves generated very intense tremors. He felt the desperation of the Vor'shak who were pressing to be released and an intense cold on the back of his neck, with the anxiety that, at any moment, the cold edge of some sharp weapon could impact him if the Vor'shak who were protecting him were defeated.

The keys fell several times to the floor, slipping from his sweaty and trembling hands, but with perseverance, Clarke managed to find the key that would open the first cage and more Vor'shak came out of it to join the fight. Some managed to grab weapons and confront the guards, but others were wounded or killed in the process. There were still more reinforcements needed to take control of the camp. Without wasting any more time, Clarke moved to the next fullest. He still didn't want to open Rex's cage, because he knew that as long as Rex was in the cage he wouldn't have to fight and put himself at risk.

Clarke ran and managed to open the next cage. With each Vor'shak that came out of it, it was a great relief and a weight off his shoulders, with this, his pulse improved and he could open the next one with more agility and speed. The camp was getting closer and closer to falling under the control of Elliott and the Vor'shak who were prisoners.

When finally, Clarke had opened almost all the cages, a greater silence could be noticed in the camp, buried among a few sounds of battle, groans of pain and sighs of the agitated breath of all those who had been involved in the bloody revolt. Clarke approached the last cage and there he could see his friend Rex who was beginning to regain consciousness after all the commotion of the battle. Upon managing to open this cage, the last Vor'shak came out and Clarke entered it to approach Rex and give him a strong hug.

—I'm so sorry, friend, excuse me for not listening to you and letting them capture us. I'm going to get you out of here now. Are you okay? — Clarke said honestly and worried about his friend's condition.

—I'm fine Clarke, a bit of a headache, but I don't really understand what's going on. Did you cause this revolt? What do we do?

—It seems everything is starting to be under control, I managed to get us out of here with the help of an elf. You be calm, follow me and I'll explain.

So, Clarke explained to Rex what had happened during this time that he was unconscious and what the next plan was to lead this group of Vor'shak together with Elliott, to Asher's base, stop him and return to the remains of the machine to rebuild it.

When the battle ended, many of the guards lay dead on the sand and others submitted to the mercy of the Vor'shak who awaited Elliott's new orders, who was located on a table in the center of the camp, covered in blood from the battle, a dagger in one hand and the bag with blue crystals in the other — Attention everyone! This camp has been liberated thanks to the actions of the great Elliott and the Vor'shak who helped me. All the loot you find will be yours, but I warn you! If you think that's all this revolt and violence could offer you, it's nothing but crumbs. There's more, much more! In the base of the leader of this group of aggressors who had us captured. If you accompany me to teach him a lesson he will never forget, riches like these blue crystals I have in my hands and much more will be accessible to you. What do you say? Let's defeat Asher and take his treasure! — Elliott ended his words with his fist raised showing a lot of energy and confidence. However, the Vor'shak were still reserved about following an elf.

Among the crowd that remained silent, one of the sturdiest Vor'shak with battle-worn features stepped forward and said — You speak well, elf, but the Vor'shak are not fooled by weak words, you don't deserve that I follow you to any...

At that moment Elliott interrupted the Vor'shak by throwing the knife he had in his hand and landing a precise blow in his right eye, where the entire blade of the weapon was buried and left the Vor'shak stiff on the ground.

All the other Vor'shak looked at each other. Clarke was also shocked by the impression of how Elliott reacted to that comment from the Vor'shak, but, a few seconds after this stunned silence, all the Vor'shak raised their arms and shouted excitedly — Yes! That's the way, for the treasure, for revenge and the glory of battle we will follow you, Elliott!

Elliott smiled knowingly and got down from the table, taking a cloth and wiping the blood from the battle off him; he approached Clarke and said — Very well, you handled yourself correctly to open the cages and make the plan work, now, if you stay with me, we will go immediately where Asher is, it's far away, near the village of Hardwind, but it will be better to surprise him before he finds out that we escaped and with the help of these crystals, it won't be any problem to get there quickly and without suffocating from the heat.

Clarke nodded, agreeing with Elliott's logic, besides, Rex at his side supported him and with that huge group of Vor'shaks, it seemed like a pretty feasible plan.

And so, Clarke began his march in the middle of the night, along with a fearless Elf, Rex, and a large number of Vor'shaks. They would be arriving at the village of Hardwind by dawn. The team felt refreshed from sleeping all those hours in the cage and although Clarke had barely rested because he was on alert, he was quite motivated to settle these matters and be able to return with his Zira team to assemble the new machine if time still allowed it, as eight months had already passed and he knew that without the machine or the plans, everything would have to go very well to manage to build it before the year that Dr. Lee had set ended.

Chapter 15: Bad Intentions

As dawn broke over the sands of Zal, a group composed of a Human, an Elf, a Sharq, and a large number of Vor'shaks was on its way to the village of Hardwind, where they would confront the cause of so many problems for Clarke. A subject capable of intensifying the infernal heat of the desert for the greed of money and power. He would not allow the air conditioning to be built, as he would not want any change to his way of life sponsored by the crystal monopoly. That was Asher, and his name was what occupied Clarke's mind throughout the entire walk.

Although Clarke was not a warrior, he had already thought about returning to the village of Zira first for more reinforcements, but the Vor'shaks refused to wait or share the loot with more people. In addition, Rex, despite having a very good sense of smell, could not locate the village of Zira from so far away, there was no clear trail that led them there and even less if they did not have blue crystals to withstand the immense heat for a long period. In the end, as the situation presented itself, the best thing was to follow Elliott to Hardwind, end Asher's misdeeds and return with Halsin to resume their plans.

They had been walking for a couple of hours, and around the group, several crystals had been used to cushion the heat. The signs of the city of Hardwind began to appear as they advanced through the desert, there, before the sight of the city, Elliott said to the group — We are getting closer, and now everyone knows what to do, the plan that we discussed on the way depends on everyone doing their part — at that moment he paid special attention with his gaze to the Vor'shaks.

-—Don't worry about us. Do your part and get us the crystals we're going to be paid for — one of the most corpulent Vor'shaks replied with his serpentine voice.

The group, during the night while crossing the desert, devised a plan of action. The idea was to get Asher to stop interfering with the plans of any of the group members and that, in addition, he would take responsibility for the damage caused. Elliott, who had already known the village of Hardwind, knew that this particular group could not enter without attracting the attention of the guards. For that, the Vor'shaks would split into two groups; the fastest would distract the city guards and avoid causing harm to avoid falling into enmity with the entire city. On the other hand, the second group of the strongest Vor'shaks along with Rex, Clarke and Elliott would infiltrate Asher's base and give him his due as well as ensure a good loot for everyone.

With this plan in mind and reaching the vicinity of the village, the Vor'shak divided and one group went around the sides, while another stayed behind the first dune waiting for Elliot's signal to enter the action. Elliot knew that this was a Dwarf village and rarely did a foreigner of another race enter without the company of another dwarf. The guards always followed that pattern to catch any foreigner who did not follow the customs and culture of the place.

From afar, as they approached, Clarke noticed how the guards guarding the outskirts saw them coming. The sand dunes were not exactly the best place to go unnoticed. And once you were going down the last one, it was a flat path to the city, without shadows or trees where you could hide. Clarke and Elliott walked normally, although they could already feel the dwarven crossbows pointing at them from afar.

— Act normal, Clarke, don't even think about running— Elliot murmured.

— This doesn't look good, Elliott. Maybe that way they'll let us pass without a problem — Clarke replied, a bit nervous.

— Well, that could be a good plan if it weren't for the fact that as soon as they see me, they're going to want to cut off our heads. Besides, Vor'shaks aren't accepted in the village of Hardwind unless they have a dwarven mark — said Elliott.

— How so? What do you mean they'll see you?

—It's a long story, but let's just say that I'm not welcome in Hardwind. And everyone knows that Vor'shaks are uncontrollable beasts unless you have them marked as slaves or subjects under the promise of a bounty like the mercenaries they are.

Clarke was annoyed to learn that Elliott had kept important details to himself that could complicate the plan they were about to carry out instead of solving it and said — You could have told me that, Elliott.

—You never asked. But it doesn't matter now, we're already here.

Clarke, resentful, decided that it was too late to turn back and obviously felt uncomfortable to focus on the moment. He noticed that Rex, who was usually very talkative, was also very quiet and attentive to the situation.

The three of them found themselves near the village and in front of a guard who approached them and said —Hey you three, elf, sharq, and human, what are you doing in Hardwind? Wait a moment...- The guard stared at Elliott, scrutinizing him.

At that moment, from the side, one of the Vor'shaks slid quickly, like a shark emerging from under the sand, and attacked the guard. At the same time, in other places and to other guards, the same surprise was heard at the hands of the group of Vor'shaks who were in charge of the distraction.

—Just in time - Elliott said as he made a "see you later" gesture to the Vor'shak and guided Clarke and Rex through the city.

The Vor'shak quickly performed a neck lock on the guard, which left him unconscious but alive, and then submerged back under the sand to continue his work of distraction.

As they moved through the alleys of the village, Elliott said— That guy Asher is a powerful man, but with shady business, his base is in the worst part of the city. I know that one well. Follow my lead, Clarke.

Several guards could be heard running through the alleys with their heavy armor behind the Vor'shaks, but for some strange reason, they had not activated the alarms.

—It's strange that they haven't activated the alarms - Clarke said curiously.

—These Dwarves are very proud, they would never activate their alarms for a few lizards running around. Hopefully, when we give the signal for the other group to reach Asher's base, the city guards will already be in other neighborhoods chasing the other Vor'shaks.

Most likely they will try to catch them without sounding the alarms. - replied Elliott looking between alleys as they advanced cautiously.

Finally, they reached an area that seemed to be a large workshop for distributing all kinds of crystals. There were many loading carts that were being dismantled and loaded with boxes bearing the seal of a mountain of ashes with the word "Asher". Apparently, he was a very proud man of his business and marked everything on his property, including the creatures that worked for him.

The small group had to be very careful, now the presence of city soldiers was very low but Asher's private security, mainly occupied by Orcs and dwarves, made a direct attack without the element of surprise unthinkable. First they had to find out if Asher was present and where.

Elliott found the situation very difficult, almost everywhere a pair of eyes was looking around. However, the elf's cunning allowed him to devise a plan — Clarke, I see that the only way to get to the central building will be by the rooftops, you and I will go that way, for Rex that will be impossible, but don't worry. Here nobody will pay attention to a solitary sharq, so Rex, stay within our sight so that you can assist us if we need it.

Rex nodded and proceeded to walk naturally within a clear range of vision to signal his two companions of the patrols.

Elliott, who was leading the way, guided Clarke through the easiest areas to climb and access the rooftops. Clarke noticed how the elf was a natural climber, making the physical effort of climbing up small ledges of the stones that decorated the buildings look easy. Clarke struggled to grip properly and not slip, but, luckily, Elliott was aware and helped him at all times. Apparently, this cunning elf was not entirely selfish or disinterested as he seemed.

Once on the rooftops, there were no guards up there, so they only had to move crouched and make sure they were not seen from below.

Between jumps and quick movements, the two managed to reach the central building, this was huge and had two floors that were marked in the decoration of the building with a border of stone slabs. Elliott, seeing them, knew how to take advantage of them as they had enough space for their feet. In this way, the duo set out to walk along the wall of the second floor, leaning on these slabs and observing the interior of the building from the different windows.

Through the windows they could see that the interior was a large crystal distribution warehouse, inside, there were very busy packaging lines with workers and guards. None of them seemed to be Asher because most of them had slave marks and other common clothes, the guards wore uniforms and as far as Elliott knew, this guy Asher was a vain person who liked to show off his power based on his riches. So identifying him should not be a problem.

The two infiltrators continued searching from window to window very carefully so as not to fall or attract attention. Behind them, Rex from below, was watching if anyone discovered them to quickly alert them.

After a couple of windows, the duo managed to find a window from where Clarke could observe something that caught his attention. He saw Asher talking to a woman with a covered face. They were sitting facing each other with a table in between. Without being discovered, he set out to listen, giving Elliott a signal not to make a noise.

—The village has returned to calm again, no rumors or questions have been heard about the team that was lost in the fire. For now, everyone believes that what was burned under the fire were electrical distribution machines and crystals that were stored. In addition, the dwarves of Halsin are no longer around. And I imagine you've already taken care of the two loose ends, haven't you?— said the woman.

—Of course, as always, I took care of the dirty work and assembled a group of subjects to ambush them. Right now, they must be being sold for the lowest price to the farthest place in the desert. I don't understand why you insisted so much that I not kill them, it would have been faster — said Asher speaking frivolously.

—You don't know them, they may have been a nuisance, meddling in matters they shouldn't have, but Rex and Clarke are not bad people and I feel sorry that I had to do this to them, but our deal of the mines and their crystals cannot stop. You, like me, know that, in this infernal desert, there is nothing better than control and power. So as always, you can count on me to keep things as we have done all these years, Asher.

— Of course Marcela, you will continue with the control of the village of Zira, finding new workers and slaves for my mines and I will dedicate myself to protecting you and paying you well. No stupid invention is going to stop it now. And the meddlesome Halsin must be tearing his hair out. I can't imagine his face when he knows he lost all those resources and not even traces or evidence of it. Hahaha— Asher finished with a great laugh, accompanied by Marcela who was also laughing.

Clarke was completely shocked, he couldn't believe it, the person who received him in the village, with whom he had shared meals and secrets like the construction of the machine. All this time, behind her smile, she hid the intentions of not wanting to help him. It seemed that she had only accepted him because she saw him young and capable of working in the mines.

Clarke felt like a complete fool, and with all that impression at once he had been distracted and lost his balance. At that moment, Elliott reacted quickly and grabbed Clarke by his clothes, preventing him from falling, but making a lot of noise by hitting and breaking one of the slabs where they were standing.

Rex watched the accident and noticed by the noise how the nearby enemy Sharqs became aware and observed the elf and the human in a compromising situation. They had already been discovered.

—What the hell is wrong with you, Clarke? Don't get distracted, Asher is going to escape before we can do anything.

Elliott looked out the window and realized how Asher and Marcela were standing up, alert, and activating all the alarms in the room. Immediately, all the workers and guards took up their weapons and followed their security protocols, which consisted of neutralizing the threat.

Clarke composed himself and watched as Rex, amid all the commotion, looked at him nervously and ran out of the place, being chased by a couple of hostile Sharqs.

— Now what, Elliott?

— Well, since we've reached this situation, I'll give the signal. I'll follow you, covering your back, and we'll catch Asher. He's no warrior, he's a guy who's too used to the good life, he won't be a challenge for you to catch and give him a good lesson. We'll take whatever we find. The Vor'shak warriors will create a good chaos and distraction for us.

Said and done, the elf put two fingers inside his mouth and whistled with great force, the almost deafening sound reached several blocks away and the Vor'shaks that were outside the place ran to their position ready to fight to the death against whoever opposed them.

Clarke, a little stunned by the loud sound, broke the window with a battle hammer they had given him and, together with Elliott, they entered the room where Asher and Marcela were.

—It can't be, Clarke, you're okay! How did you get here?— Marcela said, very surprised.

—Stop playing games Marcela! I already know who you really are and what your plans were. What a disappointment. You don't even think about the well-being of your people or the future of your daughter.

—Clarke, don't come telling me about disappointments if you're a foreigner who has never known the reality of this world, what it's like to grow up in it, depending on a crystal so coveted that people outside the order that believes in the village kill each other every day for a small fragment. You don't know the sacrifices I made to be where I am and I would never allow anything or anyone to put them at risk. Saraí lives a life of privilege thanks to me. You should have stayed in your world, for your own good — After that, she gave a signal to Asher who opened a hatch under their feet and several armed guards came out of it.

—I suppose now, Marcela, you won't object to me killing these poor wretches — Asher said with a smile.

—No, just make sure it's quick and clean. There can't be any trace of this outside of here — Marcela said in a firm voice, but the moment she saw Clarke, she looked at the floor, avoiding eye contact.

—Elliott, I suppose you foresaw this in your plan as well, didn't you?— Clarke said nervously, while he was on guard with his battle hammer raised and close to the elf.

—The reinforcements must be arriving soon — Elliott murmured as he held his short swords drawn and ready for action.

At that moment, Asher's guards attacked first, launching slashing blows with their swords. Elliott, who was very fast and athletic, blocked both blows with his two swords, protecting himself and Clarke, whom he looked at with a serious face and urged to counterattack.

So, Clarke set out to hit with his hammer as he did when he had to remove old air machines that were on an old concrete block, hitting these blocks with all his strength with the hammer. In this same way he managed to hit one of the guards who was knocked unconscious by the impact.

—Well done Clarke! go and catch Asher, give him his lesson, find out where he keeps his safe and leave the rest of the guards to me. Go! — said the elf energetically, giving a deep cut to the other guard who fell unconscious. However, more and more guards were starting to arrive.

At that moment, Asher decided to start running through a back door that he had in his office and Marcela to go down the hatch from where the guards came.

Clarke jumped around the room to avoid the confrontation with the guards, moving over the table in the middle of the room and jumping from it towards the door where Asher was fleeing, however, one of the tallest guards, an Orc, managed to grab him and throw him to the floor.

Clarke rolled and with his hammer raised blocked a blow from the axe that this orc had. The impact was such that the wooden handle of Clarke's hammer was stuck to the axe and when the orc lifted it, he lifted Clarke's hammer with it and Clarke who was firmly attached to it.

Elliott quickly came to Clarke's rescue, but other guards had blocked his way and wouldn't let him pass without first facing death.

The orc roared with fury as he grabbed Clarke by the neck with his free hand and strangled him while lifting him into the air. Clarke struggled uselessly while trying to hold onto the orc's arm so as not to bear all his weight on his neck and at the same time kicked out, but his kicks were not very effective.

Elliott noticed that Clarke was in trouble, but he found himself was also in a tight spot. He was taking more hits than he could block and already had a few bruises and cuts caused by the various weapons his opponents had. Luckily, and suddenly, the Vor'shak who were waiting for the signal finally arrived at the place and entered the building in all possible ways and places, including the windows of the room that began to break and give way to these reptilian beings.

At that moment, Elliott could afford to throw one of his two swords in the direction of the orc who was strangling Clarke and managed to land the blow on his neck, cutting an artery. Immediately, the orc released Clarke who fell to the ground coughing and gasping for air as if he couldn't hold on for even a second longer, he was at his limit. But, Clarke, although quite shaken, was determined, he couldn't afford to lose Asher. He hadn't come this far to lose this opportunity.

Clarke got up with the orc's axe and found himself facing another one of the guards, he set out to run in the direction where Asher had run and to get rid of the guard, he threw the weapon at him with all his strength. It didn't deal a fatal blow, but it did manage to hit with enough force to stun him and run over him.

The critical situation had changed, now all the guards were busy battling in the chaos against the Vor'shak who were also skilled warriors.

Among the different corridors, Clarke began to see Asher in front of him. This guy wasn't very athletic and was even a bit overweight, so he hadn't run very far and, in passing, with the little he had run, he was already showing signs of exhaustion.

Clarke quickened his pace with the impetus of victory and as if he were a football player tackling the opposing team's player before he could score a touchdown.

Clarke propelled himself with all his strength and caught up to the dwarf who was just running in front of a door that opened from the impact and carried them falling down some stairs that led to the exterior.

Clarke hadn't seen where the path behind the door led until it was too late and he found himself with Asher, falling down the stairs and rolling into the building's outdoor patio.

They rolled down at least 15 steps and landed on the sandy ground of the patio, where several Vor'shak were fighting the guards. Clarke, on the floor and badly beaten, tried to get up while watching Asher who was in the same condition.

Full of adrenaline, Clarke began to rise, but a great electrifying pain left him paralyzed. This pain came from his right hand which appeared to have been fractured in the fall. He definitely couldn't put any weight on it. However, even so, Clarke wouldn't let Asher escape, who had already gotten up, panting and quite tired, but showing a determination to escape.

Clarke managed to stand up, trembling and enduring immense pain, and shouted — You're not getting away, Asher! I won't let you. This pain is nothing compared to the pain of fire burning your body, your dreams, and your future. You'll pay for this!

—What's wrong with you, human? You're completely crazy! Stay away from me! This was never personal, it was just business — Asher said as he ran clumsily.

Clarke continued to run after him, letting out a loud scream to face the pain and help himself muster the strength to rise and grab Asher with his left hand, whom he grabbed by the back of his clothes and with one leg brought him down to the ground. There, Clarke got on top of Asher, with his legs trapping Asher's arms between them and the dwarf's torso. There he landed a solid left hook on Asher's face that left him with blurred vision and completely shook him up.

—Don't you ever again interfere with projects that help people! —Clarke said, then landed another forceful blow with the only hand he had left to hit —Don't you ever cross my path or my plans again! —and with one more left hook, Clarke said — You'll be responsible for paying me back for everything you took from me and for more than funding the project again!

Asher didn't respond, as he lay on the ground under the pressure that Clarke was exerting on his body. But after the third blow he received and hearing Clarke's words, the dwarf began to laugh.

At that same moment, in the surroundings of the building and the patio, alarms began to sound and several guards, not Asher's, but from the city of Hardwind began to arrive riding their mounts ready to stop the chaos.

Upon hearing those alarms, all the Vor'shak that were able to move began to flee the place. Some dropped their weapons in retreat, and others left the building with bags and boxes full of crystals that they had looted. Among those subjects fleeing the building, Clarke managed to spot Elliot who was carrying a large bag of crystals and managed to make eye contact with him, waving goodbye to Clarke and also fleeing the scene.

— Your luck has run out, human, all your allies have abandoned you, and the city guards will believe me more than you, since you arrived uninvited from a dwarf and caused all this commotion. Whether you like it or not, I've won — said Asher, bloodied but with a smile.

Clarke continued to look around with a great feeling of hopelessness that grew with each second. He realized that he had been left practically alone and that the guards were beginning to surround him. At these moments, he didn't know who he could count on as allies, and it was clear that Asher showed no sign of remorse.

Out of desperation and with the need to resolve his situation, Clarke quickly got up from Asher and began to run to escape from the guards. But his run was interrupted by an abrupt pull on his right foot. Asher had thrown one of his gold chains like a lasso at his leg and had managed to knock Clarke down, who fell on his already fractured right arm. This caused Clarke immense pain and he couldn't help but scream as he writhed from the impact.

—Oh yes! Now who's laughing last, Clarke? I don't usually enjoy myself at the expense of my adversaries, but I must admit that you've been an unexpected and very funny one. You have nowhere left to run.

Clarke trembled with pain but knew he had to free himself and flee before it was too late. He tried to stand up, but his numb body barely responded.

As he looked up, searching for an escape, he noticed that Marcela was watching him from a corner. Apparently, she had remained on the sidelines of the chaos to escape after things had calmed down.

Clarke was filled with rage, but also the pain of his fractured arm was stunning him greatly. He was surrounded by the guards with each passing second. So with a great impulse that he took convincing himself to give "one last effort," he managed to stand up and start running. But it was useless. The guards threw several nets at him, and when they hit him, they knocked him down to the ground again.

—You arrived just in time, guards —Asher said with a cheerful expression, as if the wounds and blows he had received didn't bother him in the slightest —This human was the leader of the group of mercenaries who attacked my compound. Apparently, they wanted to disrupt part of the city's crystal distribution, and unfortunately for me, they managed to do so. I recommend torturing this human so that he can reveal where his group is as soon as possible— It was clear that he enjoyed the situation he had put Clarke in.

—Stop, guards, I'm innocent! — Clarke said before being interrupted.

—Shut up! human — said the guard — Everything you say will be used against you in the Supreme Court of Hardwind. Any offense against the city will be punished by death.

The guards proceeded to pick up Clarke and put shackles on him to arrest him. However, at that moment, the guards were interrupted by a shout approaching.

—Stop! That human is under my protection and care. I have higher orders that allow me to take charge of him.

When Clarke turned to see who it was, he felt the support of his friend Rex who had run up to him and was leaning near his legs —Calm down, Clarke, I brought help as soon as I sensed your scent. I apologize for taking so long and leaving you alone. You look horrible.

Clarke knelt down as he could under the nets to hug Rex, and leaned on him a little because he was completely exhausted. He could see that the voice that was looking out for him was Halsin, who was with Helmir, Björn, Balh, Harold, and Manny.

—As you can see, here I have a letter that clearly states that the human Clarke is my guest, and he can accompany me before appearing at his trial —Halsin said while showing the letter to one of the guards —But, on the other hand, I possess a warrant from the Supreme Court that demands the arrest of Asher for treason against the dwarven guild and the city of Hardwind, as well as that of the human Marcela for her collaboration in activities that directly affect one of the members of the court and the entire guild.

—That can't be! There is no evidence to reach such conclusions. I refuse — said Asher, who was about to resist arrest by the guards, but was quickly subdued and handcuffed.

Marcela saw this situation with terror and began to run through the alleys of the city. Björn, who saw her run, shouted to the guards to catch her, and in a few minutes, they found her and arrested her.

Halsin approached Clarke who was extremely exhausted from the blows and the pain of his wounds, and helped him to his feet — Clarke, I apologize for the delay, after what happened we didn't know where you were and we assumed the worst. But we've taken care of this now and we'll explain it to you later. First, let me take you to a healer.

They quickly placed Clarke on a stretcher, and he, who was exhausted, felt a sense of relief as he saw Asher and Marcela being detained against their will. It seemed that, despite how things had turned out, justice had been done. Perhaps now he could build his desired air machine before the deadline of the last 4 months of the year.

Chapter 16: Guardian Angel

Clarke woke up that night in the bed of a healer's house. A dwarf was tending to his right arm that had suffered a severe fracture in multiple bones. Apparently, thanks to a healing crystal, the bones had been put back in place without the need for surgery and he only needed to heal with an immobilizer. — Excuse me, how long will I have to use the immobilizer on my right arm? — Clarke asked, worried about not being able to continue his project with his own hands.

—Hello Clarke, it's good to see you awake. Halsin brought you in, very worried about your health. Luckily your arm will heal, but it will take a couple of months for you to move it freely and a few more months for you to be able to carry weight or do heavy work with it.

Clarke felt a great frustration at hearing that, as it condemned him to not being able to work at maximum performance in a machine that had to be built from scratch and in record time.

— Don't make that long face, Clarke, when you heal correctly you will be as good as new. Besides, there is someone who has been waiting for you and is eager to see you awake, let me go tell him — the healer got up from her chair and went to a door that led to a waiting room, from there, Rex entered running with great joy to see Clarke.

— Clarke! You're awake! It's so good to see you recover so quickly and that everything has turned out well. It's really amazing how since I've been with you we've survived all kinds of situations, I don't know if you bring me luck or bad luck, but I'm glad to be with you again.

Clarke laughed a little at Rex's comments who stood above the bed on his two legs showing his joy and closeness to Clarke — Well, I don't know if this can be called good luck, Rex, but I'm also glad to have had you with me in all these moments. By the way...— Clarke changed his tone of voice to a more serious one — What do you know about Asher and Marcela? What happened to them and how did you manage to arrest them?

— Well, Clarke, right now they are being held in the Hardwind dungeon, they are awaiting their trial. I don't know the exact details, but Halsin can tell you more about that when you leave here and we go to his house. Luckily, I managed to get them as soon as all the alarms sounded and when he found out that you were in danger, of the ambush they gave us outside of Zira, he didn't hesitate to gather his people and notify the authorities. That's when we arrived at the rescue, apparently at just the right moment because it seemed that they were about to arrest you and give you a quick trial for foreigners where if no one from Hardwind opposes, they cut off your head in less time than I can count.

Clarke put his hand to his neck and swallowed hard. The truth is, at that moment, the whole scenario indicated that he had done something against the city and its members. Luckily, Halsin has great influence and has evidence to prove which side was fighting against the law.

With many more questions and without wanting to wait, Clarke got up to meet with Halsin. The healer gave the final touches to the immobilizer on his arm and let Clarke go with Rex.

— We must go straight to Halsin's house, you're still on parole until the trial proves that you are innocent and Marcela and Asher guilty — Rex said as they walked.

When they arrived at Halsin's house, they found Helmir who was eating some meat fillets and beer. — Clarke! You recovered! I didn't expect anything less. You've always surprised me. And in a good way for being a human. Come and sit with me, there's meat and beer for everyone.

Clarke who was hungry and noticed how the meat fillet of whatever animal it was, looked tender and juicy did not hesitate to join Helmir. — Thanks for the invitation Helmir, I really had a little more than a day without eating. By the way, I hadn't seen you for several months. How have you been?

—Relax, help yourself. You're right Clarke, we hadn't seen each other for months. I've been very busy working on a project that Halsin had me in charge of here in Hardwind, I'm sure Halsin will want to show it to you later. And how do you feel? It was so unexpected to find out that you had cornered the bastard Asher, I would have liked to give him a few good punches too.

—Well...— In that moment, Clarke was about to respond to Helmir, but he noticed Halsin entering through the front door, with several parchments in his hands.

—Clarke! How good to see you recovered! And it's good that you're eating, nothing worse for healing than an empty stomach. Feel free to eat whatever you want —Halsin approached Clarke, checking his wounds and said to him —You have proven to be not only very intelligent but also a brave warrior, Clarke. I never expected that you would manage to escape alone from the hands of Asher's henchmen and at the same time bring a group of mercenaries to his door and corner him. The truth is, I already had my suspicions and an investigation about him. For years I have known that he was in murky business, but I never had proof that it affected the activities of Hardwind until you arrived.

—How long have you known about Asher and Marcela? Did you expect them to attack us and destroy the air machine project?— Clarke asked curiously, stopping eating the juicy steak that Helmir gave to him.

—Well, Clarke, now that you're recovered and, in my house, I think it's the perfect time to tell you everything. Since I met you at Marcela's house, you seemed like a curious fellow. For years I've been thinking of a way to help my community and its allies live a better life. Many of the dwarves in Hardwind have a pretty privileged life if you compare it to almost all the inhabitants of Zal, and since I was little, this life with crystals at my convenience helpers to attend to me and everything I wanted was very normal for me. But when I discovered the fate of others, I couldn't help but be moved. Now that I'm the head of my clan, one of the most important members of the dwarven guild order. I've been looking for a way to address the scarcity of crystals and help people not die of heat, creating safe and cool spaces for communities. That desire couldn't materialize because I couldn't find a way to make it possible until you told me about the air conditioning machine. Imagine being able to be in the heat of the day and enter a building that is cool and cold, that you can store things without being exposed to the terrible heat, deal with not needing a crystal every half day to cool yourself indoors. That, my friend, is a magic that people have dreamed of for generations. Although it is a wonderful invention, there are people who live and enjoy at the expense of the suffering of others, that's where you find people like Asher, who has a large network of slaves and distribution of crystals throughout Zal, for him, that the crystals become scarce translates into a price increase and greater power. He wasn't interested in helping anyone and would be capable of watching the world burn just by maintaining his status. I knew that a guy like that wouldn't hesitate to destroy any invention like the one you were planning. That's why I sent you to Marcela's, so that you could work a little more out of his reach and in secret. But much to my regret, I didn't expect Marcela to betray me and be working with Asher.

— The truth is, I don't think anyone expected it, I still can't believe it completely — Rex replied a little sadly.

—Well, there were signs, but maybe we didn't want to see them — said Halsin and continued —The moment you left Hardwind with my kura full of the materials to start the construction, a Vor'shak attacked you, luckily you defeated it and managed to reach the village of Zira. That Vor'shak had to be sent from Hardwind by someone who knew you could be carrying valuables and who underestimated you for seeing that you were not warriors. When I heard about it, I sent several of my subjects to track the corpse, but they found nothing. Then I found out from Rex, that when you told him about the attack on Marcela, she sent her own Sharq to recover the body of the reptilian, surely she wanted to hide any mark that linked the attack to her or to Asher. It wasn't until later, when you were working on the project, in the time that Helmir and Björn were helping you with the first steps. I heard from them.

—Yes, I noticed together with my brother Björn, that the guards that Marcela had to watch the perimeter of where we worked, knew more than they should about our work in that workshop and were constantly seen more attentive to us than to the surroundings. If they were Marcela's most trusted subjects, they acted that way on her orders, because it is difficult for them to want to betray her and us on their own —Said Helmir, finishing chewing a piece of meat and added — It's that even the solar metal that Halsin sent them, Björn told me all the trouble they had to weld it, the only thing that fits in my head about the reason for this was that Marcela who was in charge with her people of dismounting it from the kura and storing it, surely modified it at some point, being her capable of being the only one in welding it. Perhaps she did it to make sure that the machine was built under a time set by her while planning with Asher how to stop them cleanly and without suspicion.

—It was at that moment that I decided, together with Helmir, that I should return to Hardwind when you needed materials and stay here working on a project of mine while I sent more help with Balh, Manny and Harold. From then on we tracked every suspicious movement. But with special discretion, we didn't want to raise suspicions and lose the opportunity to discover the spies. Then, the night Harold saw some guards exchanging information, he tried to confront them and they took him captive. The guards were human and they didn't kill him because they didn't want the dwarven guild to get fully involved because of the death of one of their own, that would greatly affect Marcela's freedom of action in Zira. Without a doubt they wanted to buy time. They already knew clearly that you were about to finish the machine and that all the plans, tools and materials you had with it in that single building. From then on, the ambush seemed like the perfect plan and, boy did it work! They took you and everyone involved out of the village and gave the perfect time for Marcela with Asher's lackeys to set the workshop on fire, making sure to erase all trace of the project. At that point you were the only one missing. And they would know that, upon returning, you would look for the culprit. That project was too important to you. I would dare to say that with the impetus you showed in it, you would have given your life to save it.

Clarke was with no words and with the steak on his plate getting cold and with flies. He realized that Halsin was right and that at that moment when he ran into the fire, he was willing to burn again just to rescue that machine that was no longer there, and that now sitting at that table, he realized that it was not worth his life. His life was worth more and being alive gave him another chance to create it.

Halsin continued — When you came running to the village and saw the building on fire, Marcela pretended to try to save the workshop, but the fire was already unstoppable. They baited you by presenting you with a supposed culprit who was fleeing and you followed them out of the village as Asher and Marcela predicted. Their plan had worked until they caught you. They didn't expect to see you again. There, I'm not sure exactly what they were going to do with you.

—They were going to sell us as slaves to some trafficker or mine boss on the outskirts of Zal, very far away to make sure we didn't come back — Clarke said—Luckily we managed to meet an elf named Elliott who had a plan to rob Asher.

—Elliott? That's curious, I don't know the guy, but from what I see, he got what he wanted and left the place before the guards arrived. Anyway. A guy like Asher has more than one enemy, although these rarely end up well. Luckily for you, that unexpected ally allowed you to escape and surprise Asher and Marcela with a group of mercenaries at their doors. It was the biggest loose end of them all. They were surely meeting to close the case of the air and consider themselves victorious. Once Rex came running and told me what had happened and the situation you were in, I knew what to do. The puzzle was coming together. And the icing on the cake was seeing Marcela in the same place. How could she be in Hardwind if the direct invitation was from a dwarf? She had already written me a letter about everything that had happened with you, Rex and the machine, we had nothing to discuss and less so suddenly. She was there, near Asher's building! Definitely to meet with him!

—Yes, before I went in, I heard them talking to Asher and celebrating that their plan had gone perfectly until they discovered us and everything ended in chaos. Luckily they didn't escape — said Clarke.

—Exactly! And now we have all the proof to make sure they spend a retirement behind bars thinking about all the harm they were willing to cause for their own selfishness— said Halsin with excitement showing great joy.

Clarke, on the other hand, was happy to know everything that had happened and how things ended, with justice prevailing, but he was also a little sad — Yes, I'm also glad we got out of this well, but I'm so sorry to have lost the machine and all the diagrams and parts related to it. The truth is it will be very hard to build a new one if it is possible...

Halsin placed his hand on Clarke's shoulder and with a huge smile said — I have something to show you, friend. Finish eating and come with me.

Clarke took his last bites and drank the glass of water in one gulp. Then he stood up and got ready to follow Halsin.

The group walked out of the house and headed to one of the ends, almost to the outskirts of the city, where there was a large building covered by several stone walls and several dwarven guards on the outskirts. When they entered, Helmir took the lead and opened some large sliding doors that led to a mechanical workshop. There, Clarke observed something that left him speechless and shook his world.

Inside the building was a very similar replica of his magical air conditioning machine, there were copies of the schematics and diagrams, the pipes were already welded and it was practically very close to the almost finished state of the machine that was incinerated by the fire in the village of Zira.

—I can't believe it! It's a copy of the machine I was building! Halsin, Helmir, how did you do it? — Clarke said with great joy, jumping for joy. So much so that Rex had to urge him to stop so he wouldn't get hurt.

—As you know, Clarke, when Helmir returned to the village, we already had high suspicions that the project was in danger so we decided to be extra careful and replicate the machine here. Besides, since I am the main financier of the project, I wanted a replica to be able to use and benefit the city. As you know, one of the reasons you are free after having entered a large group of mercenaries into the city and having assaulted the lands of a dwarf, is not only because I am influential or because your target was a criminal, but also because I plan to present this finished project as a patented invention of the dwarven guild. It will continue to help people, but it will be under the labor, financing and control of my people. So, since you are involved in something so important, you will be treated with special care as an ally of all.

Clarke was silent for a moment, he realized that in the end, his project was still not entirely his own and that it would not be freely accessible either. But thinking about it better, he compared the situation with the different companies that design their own air conditioning models in Florida and the truth is that the work and materials used in the design of these machines was high, and it was better to leave them in the hands of professionals who could maintain them, create them efficiently and make them safe. Without a doubt, in what he could think of and remember. That it fell into Halsin's hands was one of the best things that could have happened. 'I'm glad you thought about building a replica. I can see how this project will come to life soon and help a large number of people. I trust you to make it accessible and that the greatest number of people can enjoy this and many future replicas that are built in the villages.

—You can count on it, Clarke! It makes me happy to know that now that you know everything that happened, you still want to finish the project. I know that there are only a few details that I couldn't put together with Helmir to achieve what you had done in Zira and to turn it on. We'll leave that for later, after the trial where you will testify with Rex and help me with all the evidence to imprison Asher, Marcela and all their allies.

The group, after having seen the machine and making sure that everything was in its place, closed the workshop and headed to Halsin's house where they would spend the night. Clarke was finally able to sleep in a cloth bed, in his own room, knowing that he would have the time to finish the machine. That night, peacefully and calmly as he had not done for many nights, he slept with a big smile on his face.

Chapter 17: The Final Stretch

The trial took place the following day before the Supreme Dwarven Court of Hardwind. The evidence gathered by Halsin's team over all these months and that found at the time of raiding Asher's base and Marcela's house were decisive for the sentence that these two would receive. Clarke, along with Rex and all those affected, testified before the court and after a long review process by all the members of the jury, they sentenced Asher to a chain of 100 years and after his release, the impossibility of directing mining operations again, among others.

Marcela, who reluctantly accepted the reality of the situation, had the same sentence, but unlike the dwarves who live close to half a millennium, for Marcela it meant being imprisoned for the rest of her life. The dwarves did not distinguish their laws and especially with someone who affected from outside of Hardwind directly with their order and activities.

At the time of the sentence, despite everything that had happened, Clarke felt sorry for her. Especially for her daughter Saraí who was only 8 years old and had no known father. Thinking that she was alone made him feel bad and it was reflected on his face. Halsin who, during that moment, was sitting next to him in the courtroom, put his hand on his shoulder and said — Don't worry, Clarke, I'm not happy about Marcela's fate either, although I am a supporter of justice and I was also a genuine friend of Marcela, although under a lie. I'm worry about her daughter who has nothing to do with this. I will make sure that she is under my protection as her uncle, which is how she has always made me feel. I will take care of her and guide her with the ideals that she has always had of growing up as the successor leader of Zira under the principles of helping her people; but without sacrificing the well-being of others.

Clarke felt a huge relief at hearing those words from Halsin, and together they left the court, with all the adversaries to their project arrested and sure to continue progressing in it. Asher and Marcela would not be the last to impose themselves on the progress and revolution of this invention, but there was no longer any imminent threat that they had to worry about. Clarke and his team were with their heads held high and looking with a smile at the future that was materializing.

In the following days, Clarke resumed work on the machine in Hardwind. He still had his arm immobilized, but he had the entire team of Halsin and Rex to support him. He delegated and directed the members to carry out the remaining work on the construction of the air. The atmosphere in the workshop was cheerful, jovial, and just as Clarke had always imagined it would be when he had to lead a team. Clarke couldn't help but remember his experience with the Coolforever technicians and how at that time he didn't trust his members for the projects, delaying the work and even generating more problems by not doing so. He realized how very wrong he was and was happy that he had managed to change. Suddenly, not being able to do things by himself didn't bother him so much. He knew that behind every hammer blow, every well-made weld, and every good job done, he was part of it. As a leader, he was part of the successes and failures. So, what better than to be part of both situations, than to always push to go for victories and goals achieved?

Several weeks passed and finally the machine was finished. The entire team that had worked on it was present and anxious when it was time to turn on the air system for the first time, everyone insisted that Clarke do it and he, with a huge smile and using his good hand, raised the power lever and the machine emitted an exciting sound that it was working and was working as it should. That whole night they celebrated and drank beer with joy. They had done it. The air conditioning machine was a reality and it worked as planned. The workshop was climatized to the desired temperature and days later they distributed the cold air to the other houses of Hardwind, the whole city was impressed and relieved, apparently, the damage of the scarce crystals was a thing of the past and life seemed to be more pleasant in the future for all its inhabitants.

In the following months, Clarke dedicated himself to working and helping Halsin's team with the maintenance processes of the machine. In future plans for the construction of more machines in other allied villages like Zira, and even mentioned designs to the others about refrigerators and freezers. The idea of drinking cold beer was something that greatly motivated the dwarves who were completely convinced with the idea.

Halsin had earned the complete leadership of Hardwind, the people saw him as a divine envoy who made the invention of air possible and Clarke was recognized as a fundamental pillar of that work. Clarke didn't mind, his mission was to bring people something that would help them in their lives and he had achieved it with help.

One day, when it was almost time to celebrate a year since he arrived in the desert, Clarke was heading in an Urka to the village of Zira, along with Rex, carrying materials to start the reconstruction of the air conditioning system.

On the way, Clarke observed the wide horizon of the desert with its surrounding dunes, while doing so, he observed something that caught his attention, it was a humanoid figure wandering alone through the desert.

— Hey Rex, do you see that guy wandering alone in the desert?

— I don't see anything Clarke, are you feeling okay? Maybe the heat is making you see things.

Clarke kept watching the figure that had stopped and was looking from afar in his direction, it looked like a human he didn't recognize.

— It's serious Rex, do you really not see it?

— I don't see it Clarke, what's more, I can't even smell it and that says there's nothing there. You should sleep a while while the kura advances to the village.

The figure that Clarke saw in the distance was becoming clearer and clearer. As he tried harder to detail the figure he saw, he realized it was a human with white hair and a white beard.

— Doctor Lee! — Clarke shouted in surprise and immediately went to get off the kura to run where Lee was.

— Clarke! What are you doing? Where are you going? — Rex said worried about Clarke's sudden reaction, and decided to follow him.

One after the other they ran over the sands, moving away a little from the kura. Clarke was impressed to see the doctor in such a remote place and exposed to the intense heat, but as he saw the doctor all clean, without sweat or reflection that the place or the conditions affected him, he doubted if he was really in front of him or if it was a mirage. Until he heard.

—You're a different man, Clarke, you've done well. I can tell by looking at you, by being in the towns and villages where you've been how you've given your best part of yourself to those around you. You must be very proud of what you've achieved.

— Doctor lee! But… What are you doing here?

—You may be right, but that would be if the calendar of your world of origin were the same as that of this world. The truth is, that in Zal, the calendar is a few days shorter and I didn't see the need to explain it to you. Doing things on time is like doing them late and the least I expected is that you would achieve it sooner. Which you did.

Clarke had a moment of silence, apparently his time in this desert world was over, he would return to his world of origin and leave everything behind. A great feeling of uncertainty invaded him at that moment, he did not know what awaited him next.

Here he had already mentally prepared the many projects to do with Halsin and his people, but at the same time, a warm memory made him feel calmer, knowing that he had given his best and had delegated the projects to a very capable team, he knew they would be fine without him. Although at that moment, his thoughts were interrupted by a voice that was speaking to him.

—Clarke, what's happening? Who are you talking to? Are you okay?

Clarke, upon hearing his voice, felt a great icy cold throughout his body. Rex, his great and only friend in years, who had saved him, cared for him, accompanied him and supported him throughout this adventure, was a citizen of Zal, of all the things and people he would leave behind, what would happen to him?

—Doctor Lee, if you're telling me that the time has come, what does it mean? Does it mean I have to return to my world? What happens to everything that stays here and the people?

—It means it's time to return to your world of origin, Clarke, it's not possible for you to stay here any longer. Your influence undoubtedly left a permanent mark on the people and lives of this world, but such an impact has a price when you are not in your universe of origin, and that is that you must return or you risk disappearing. I knew that your impact would be great and that's why I calculated a year for you to have to return. It's time. Are you ready?

Clarke heard those words and had a sudden attack of sadness, he didn't want to say goodbye to his friend Rex, he threw himself to the ground on his knees, and holding back his tears he hugged Rex tightly.

—What's wrong Clarke? Tell me what's wrong please, you're worrying me.

— Thank you for everything Rex, you've been the best friend I could have wished for. Take care of yourself please. I love you friend!— said Clarke while saying these words with a tearful voice.

Clarke's body at that moment began to sparkle and his body began to dematerialize, scattering particles that rose with the wind. Rex did not understand what was happening, he could not hear or see Doctor Lee, but he noticed how Clarke was vanishing into the air and with this he dedicated himself to shouting Clarke's name until he could not see him anymore.

Clarke's entire vision went dark and suddenly he found himself floating in space, he was in the middle of nowhere and accompanied by the twinkling of the stars in the distance, suddenly he heard Doctor Lee's voice again.

— I apologize that your farewell was so abrupt, Clarke. I see that Rex was very important to you on this journey, and I suppose you had many things to hold on to in that world. However, it was impossible for you to stay, it had to be this way.

Clarke was silent as he came to his senses and accepted what was happening. He was fighting against his denial of the facts.

— What you did in the world of Zal, what you lived during this year is not meaningless at all, Clarke. All the achievements of your invention and its consequences are very real for the people of that world and many families, people, children and other creatures will be able to live more peacefully, with a longer and fuller life as you saved them from the ravages of dying from the heat without the use of crystals. You became a hero.

—But, but what do I have left of that, Lee? It's okay to be a hero and help people, but in the world I'm going back to, nobody knows that or is going to believe me. Everything I had, I lost it. I lost my friends, home, life.

—You're right and you're wrong at the same time, Clarke. You've had all those things and more in your world of origin, the difference is that you yourself were responsible for losing them in the first place, you neglected your friends, your family, your home, health, everything for your work and not wanting to count on anyone else. But throughout this year with everything against you, you managed to find your own path of change and gain all those things that you had lost. You lived in a balance between all those things and you were much better.

— And what? Now you've taken everything away from me, Lee. You've left me with nothing!

—You're wrong, Clarke. In your home world, you still have a life, although with different challenges and difficulties than the desert, you still have a future, you still have your son Alejandro who feels more and more like he's losing his father every day. All your acquaintances know that you're an incredible air technician and although you can't practice, you have a brilliant mind to teach and delegate as the leader you always wanted to be and that you learned to be in Zal. Now you can show the world your true potential. Since I met you, I knew you were a warrior, or was I wrong? There are still people who can see your potential, but, after everything you've been through, don't you see it yet?

Clarke thought in silence about Doctor Lee's words. The truth was, if he had transformed during his stay in Zal, he remembered that time in the mines when he hit the rocks with determination to change his destiny, to change who he was, seeing himself reflected in his past as Duspathalyn, who had been his tyrannical boss in the mines. He remembered the excitement of having a future project about air and how being a good leader had brought him joy by sharing with a team that respected and appreciated him equally, transforming each achievement of his team as one of which he was also a part. He remembered his fight against Asher who had tried to stop him and attack his weak points and yet he was able to defeat him, not only with luck, but with determination, in how he fought even with his broken arm to show him that his good intentions of helping others could propel him further, to surpass his limits. The truth is, what Clarke always loved about his work was the smile of his clients, how they thanked him after repairing a machine that without it even the interior of his home could stop being a palace and become a hell.

Clarke raised his hands in front of him, while floating in space face up and watching how his experiences had marked him forever and there were still things that needed him to do them, he had his son who surely missed him and who still needed him to not fall into the same mistakes as his father. He still had the opportunity to lead an air team and continue helping people live more comfortably in the face of the enormous heat of Florida, providing a service like no other.

Clarke heard Doctor Lee's question again, questioning whether he was a warrior or someone who runs away from difficult situations. There Clarke's pride came to the surface, he knew and had proven that he always faced difficult situations head-on, with perseverance, with determination and with pride in not being defeated, and he knew that now he had even learned to count on the support of others as well.

It was a difficult and very painful situation to say goodbye to everything he had done in Zal, but he knew that those experiences and memories accompanied him wherever he went.

—You were right, Doctor Lee, if I am a warrior, it's from the cradle. That has allowed me to achieve my goals in one way or another and along the way help many people. I know now that I am a better warrior, who thinks about his battles and his actions before doing them, using all the resources at my advantage, so I will surely have fewer failures and mistakes along the way. But, I admit that I have not been very fortunate with the challenges that I have had to face.

— Clarke, I am glad to see that you are aware of your own progress as a person. And about your challenges in life, each person faces their own, many of them you caused yourself, but you had this opportunity that I gave you to learn how to face them and now that I see you, I know that no challenge in your path has been too big for you, you have always exceeded expectations. Remember that always and now take advantage of living your life the way you really wanted, don't lose your way, and remember that, although you don't see me, I will always be supporting you and watching over you.

—Who are you, Doctor Lee?

At that moment, the space where Clarke was floating began to move like a whirlwind, everything was being sucked into a sudden black hole that was tiny and that was getting bigger and bigger as it absorbed everything in space, including Clarke. There was little he could do as he screamed and was sucked into the immense darkness.

Chapter 18: A New Man

Clarke woke up suddenly on the hospital room bed, as soon as he opened his eyes he looked around for Doctor Lee, it seemed that only a blink of an eye had passed since he was in space. He noticed that there was an extinguished incense stick on the bedside table and a voice distracted him.

— Mr. Clarke, are you alright?

Clarke noticed a man sitting in the chair near the bed, he was wearing a white coat, black hair, and glasses. By the looks of it, he must be a doctor, but he was not one he recognized.

— Excuse me, I got lost for a moment. Who are you? And where is Doctor Lee?

— Don't worry Mr. Clarke, it's normal not to be completely clear after an accident like the one you suffered. Remember that I'm here to help you, I'm the psychiatrist, Doctor Pinto. I don't think we have a Doctor Lee on the payroll. Is he someone you know?

Clarke was surprised, the incense on the table was the one that Dr. Lee had left him, and besides he had introduced himself as a psychiatrist. Clarke understood that maybe he would not see him again. It may be that Doctor Lee was a presence beyond his understanding just like his whole trip to Zal, it was an experience that he should better keep to himself.

—Yes, he is a psychiatrist I saw in a magazine, I thought he worked here, but since you're here I don't worry. I know I'm with a professional.

—Well, thank you very much, Clarke, of course, I can assure you that I, like the other doctors, are attentive so that you have your best recovery. Your treatments, therapies, and adaptation process will take time, feel free to communicate how you feel during these next few months and I will help you in whatever way I can.

Clarke realized it upon hearing the entire recovery process and he realized, he remembered that after his accident in the building where he worked, he had lost his legs and hands, apparently he no longer needed to many machines connected to him, he could speak and see, although burn scars covered part of his body. Clarke still had the feeling of feeling his hands and feet, but it was due to the effect of phantom limbs. Clarke could not help but break down and grieve for being back in that state.

—Clarke, before I go and leave you for a while before the next doctor visits you, I wanted to inform you that, during these weeks, your insurance was updated and with the CoolForever company you will have all treatment covered, prosthetics and the best professionals to help you and have a better recovery. It is going to be a challenge, but you have the best team for that. Here I leave you some books of several of our patients and how they have recovered successfully. Their stories are very interesting.

Clarke was silent as he listened to the doctor's words and his own thoughts, although he held back with all his might, a few tears escaped because of being the way he was.

The doctor left and the room was silent, Clarke had a moment of reflection, of analysis and of answering himself many questions about his life and his future.

After a few hours, the door of the room opened and a very pleasant surprise entered the room. It was Clarke's son, Alejandro.

— Dad! You woke up!— said Alejandro as he approached and touched Clarke's shoulder. He had tears on his face — Several weeks have passed and the doctors didn't know what to tell me, they told me that you were connected to machines that kept you alive and the best thing was to wait for you to show improvement. You don't know how happy I am to see you awake, dad — Alejandro wiped the tears from his cheeks with the palms of his hands.

—Son, it's so good to see you. You know your father is a warrior, here I am recovering. I told you we would watch that program you recorded, do you remember?

—Dad, do you still remember that? Of course I do, I still have it recorded so we could watch it together. But, you scared me a lot. That accident you had at work was quite serious, you're alive by a miracle. You don't know how grateful I am that that miracle intervened. —Alejandro showed tears on his cheeks again, he was struggling not to cry in front of his father, but he was very excited.

— I'm sorry for worrying you so much, son, I'm sorry for not being able to be with you more, for not answering all your calls, for all the failures I showed you of me.

—What are you saying, Dad? Don't apologize for anything, I know that work is important and you had to focus, I apologize more to you for having distracted you when you always told me that what you did was dangerous. The recorded programs and those things didn't matter that much.

—The programs themselves didn't matter, but you're wrong, son, work is important but not more than your family. I should never have neglected mine so much. And if you allow me, now I hope it's not too late to share with you again many of those things that you always called me to do with you.

—Of course, Dad! Don't even doubt it. You know that you can also count on me, and I will accompany you in your therapies and recovery, count on it!

At that moment, Clarke responded to his son with a gesture and they hugged. Clarke felt relief and enormous strength to continue, he would do it for himself and for his son.

In the following months, Clarke continued with his medications, physical therapies, therapies with his psychiatrist and even read all the books that Doctor Pinto had recommended to him.

Some time later, Clarke managed to leave the hospital with his new prosthetics, although still in a wheelchair. His son Alejandro would pick him up and pack his things to get in the car. Clarke watched him from one side of the vehicle sitting on the chair. He watched as his son listed everything with great excitement, however, it seemed that he was bringing something in the car that he wanted to show him.

—Dad, I don't know what your relationship is with a certain Doctor Lee, but he left a letter and a gift at my house for you. He was very specific about bringing it to you as soon as you were discharged from the hospital. Maybe he doesn't know you very well, but I brought it to you so you can tell me what you prefer to do with it.

Clarke got very excited when he heard the name Doctor Lee, he didn't know anything about him since he disappeared in their conversation while floating in space. What could that special gift be? Clarke became impatient and suddenly heard a sound. What he heard and observed he did not expect and left him completely speechless.

Getting out of the car and running towards him, approaching with the biggest smile of all, a brown dog with pointed ears, it reached Clarke and on its two legs stood up to hug him.

Clarke was impressed, he couldn't believe what he was seeing, the dog excitedly licked and hugged him. Clarke stroked his head and body with his stumps, imagining it was who he thought it was, until he confirmed it by reading the name on his collar, "Rex". Clarke, shocked, cried and said— Rex! Friend, what are you doing here? How is this possible? I missed you so much too!

His son Alejandro, surprised by his father's reaction who had never shown special affection for animals, approached him and said — Wow! Dad, when did you start liking dogs? That Doctor Lee must know you very well. Here, take this. With the dog there was a letter that I didn't want to read, it was only for you.

Clarke held his son's letter on his lap and began to read:

"Dear Clarke, good actions towards others leave indelible marks on their lives that make them want to be close to you. You performed many great feats in the last year, but a very special one, your first and greatest achievement was opening up to someone very special. His life was no longer going to be the same after what they lived together and his mission in the desert no longer had as much relevance as the mission he wanted and decided to accept. Rex accepted the challenge of helping you and accompanying you, regardless of not being able to return to his world, he came to this one to be with you. He can't speak here, but I'm sure that with the bond of friendship that you created. Words are superfluous. I wish you both the best and remember my last words when we last spoke. You are never alone."

Clarke finished reading the letter and was very excited, now he had great confidence about the future, he had his son closer than ever and he could count on his great friend Rex for the adventures and challenges of tomorrow.

In the coming years, Clarke would manage to recover, adapt completely to the prosthetics and open his own company with his son called

CoolForAll where he would train future technicians with the motto of giving the best service of all to his clients in Florida, Rex accompanied him as a guide dog and was part of the company's logo, and together with his son who now taught how to live the perfect balance between work and personal time, friends and family. Clarke was thus able to have a full life and enjoy it more than in previous years, now he learned new things that he had never dedicated time to, traveled and met places, helped others and became an example of overcoming and success for all the people around him who admired and appreciated him in the same way. Clarke had become a new man.

The End.

Disclaimer

This is a work of fiction that does not intend to be based on the life of any specific person. The names of people and companies do not intend to make specific mention of anyone. The only real references are the inspiration for the fabulous invention of modern air conditioning by its creator Willis Haviland Carrier. In addition to the spectacular state of Florida, the cradle where this story was born and written.

If you like this story and its message, don't forget to check out the other works of its author Manuel A. Ruiz Sosa

"The Children and the Green Dragon"

Follow me:

Tik-tok @manuel.ruizsosa.author

Instagram: manuelruizautor